Lost

and

Found

D1602477

Lost and Found
©2015 by Shelby June

Published by Piscataqua Press
An imprint of RiverRun Bookstore, Inc.
142 Fleet St.
Portsmouth, NH 03801

www.piscataquapress.com
www.riverrunbookstore.com

ISBN: 978-1-939739-95-7
Printed in the United States of America

Author's Website:
shelbyjunebooks.com

Lost and Found

a novel

Shelby June

Thank You ~ From the Heart

First and foremost, a special thank you to my family – for *everything*!
You mean the world to me, and I am determined to make you proud.

Rod Grondin Photography
Thank you for the beautiful cover – it was love at first sight!

Tiffany Brand
For getting me back to school ~ You have been a true life-long friend.

My writing classmates – Colleen, Brad, Jen, Cheyenne, Deb, Pam,
Maija
You've been with me on this journey from the start.
Dawn – The "Leader of the Pack" – Thank you!

My *sklawyers, pllc* Family
You are the best ~ Thanks for letting me follow this dream
(before 8am and after 5pm, right KKC?)

Karyn Krause Cumberland
You are a true inspiration and make me a better person. Seriously.

BNI TEAM Eppicenter - Your support and enthusiasm mean so much –
I'm glad you're with me on this yellow brick road!

The Game Night Girls – Katie, Jeannine, Diane, Karen, Julie, Melissa,
Molly

Joshua L. Greenspan, MD
Thanks for getting my head straight so I can enjoy all this!

My Content Editors – Teresa Troy, Melissa Zani, Lynne Rocheleau,
Michelle Trodella,
Terri O'Brien, and Evelyn Liston
Your feedback, edits, and suggestions have been invaluable!

"H" ~ 28 years later, you still inspire me!

My "happy place" – St. John, USVI
The most beautiful place in the world – see you soon!

My friends – old and new – you are extended family.

To every author of every book I have ever read ~ I have enjoyed your
work, your imagination, and your willingness to let me into your world and
fall in love with your characters.

Thank you to my new friends at the New Hampshire Writers Project –
wonderful people!

I would love to hear from you!
shelbyjunebooks@gmail.com

*This novel is dedicated to those affected,
both directly and indirectly, by the Holocaust
and also to those who still work so diligently
to continue to tell the story of this
heartbreaking part of our world's history.*

1

Elizabeth

There is no one to blame but me for my daughter's ignorance. Olivia does not know me, though she thinks she does. She knows I was born overseas, she knows I came to America in my twenties, got married to my beloved William and brought her into the world in my thirties. My daughter has, so far, lived a wonderful life, and now she has a family of her own.

My daughter's ignorance prevents me from being angry that she asked me to take the train to her home today. William and I walked everywhere, and if it was raining, we would take a taxi. In the heart of the city everything is close by. My daughter lives in the 'burbs' as she calls them. She and Tim moved there when she found out she was pregnant with Alexander. William and I would spend the night at her home the night before holidays, like Thanksgiving or Christmas Eve. Olivia and I would get up early, get the turkey in the oven and the rest of the meal prepared. Since William passed away several months ago, she has asked me to live with them several times. I tell her I'm not ready to leave the penthouse. I won't do it, because she lives near the woods.

Before I lost William, it was easy for me to push my past life out of my mind. Now that he is gone, I am now constantly haunted with triggers, because William isn't here to protect me. Standing beside his 6'2" frame with his arm around me I felt safe.

Olivia and I are sometimes more like sisters than mother and daughter. We are even closer since William left us, and I appreciate Tim's patience with our daily phone conversations, at least three every day, and our visits, at least three every week. I could not ask for a better son-in-law. And my grandchildren –

Alex, a freshman at NYU and Abbie, a sophomore in high school, are my pride and joy.

It is Thanksgiving Day, my first Thanksgiving without William. As I stand in front of my mirror, dressed and ready to go, I can see William in the reflection beside me. He looks so handsome, in his navy blue suit, pressed shirt, a tie Olivia had bought him, and a smile on his face. His greatest joy was spending time with his family, and he especially loved holidays. It didn't matter which one it was, as long as he was with us. I primp my hair just one more time, look up, and he is gone. He is gone from my sight, but he is always with me. His spiritual companionship gets me through one day to the next, though today will be a difficult day. He will not be there to cut the turkey. He will not be there to lead us in prayer. I will try to make this trip alone.

In the elevator, I watch the doors close. An uneasy feeling begins to churn in my stomach. I close my eyes and say a little prayer that I can do this; that I can get to Olivia's house, one step at a time. *Take a deep breath. Think of William.* The elevator doors open with a quick, soft chime of a bell. *Here I go.*

"Happy Thanksgiving, Mrs. McNamara." It is George, our door man. He is the smile that now welcomes me home and the smile that sends me on my way. "Bundle up, it's cold out there."

"George, thank you. Same to you, my friend. Family dinner later?"

"Yes ma'am, and hopefully the turkey won't be dry like last year," he says with a smile. "My daughter-in-law, she's learning – slowly."

"I will have good thoughts for you tonight, George."

"You and me both. I wish I could call someone for you, but there's no way anyone could get to you in all this chaos."

"I understand, George. I imagine it's a zoo out there."

"It sure is, since the sun came up. People love a good parade, don't they?"

"People love tradition, George. I will see you later," I say as I make my way through the revolving door. The sidewalks are lined with people, vendors pushing carts with balloons and other goodies, children on their parent's shoulders, waiting with anticipation.

The sun is shining but it's windy and cold – one might say a typical November day in New York City. I clutch my scarf with my right hand to prevent the wind reaching my neck, my left hand clutching the top of my coat. *I'm coming, Olivia, I'm coming.*

I have now walked several blocks and reach the stairway down to the subway. I have never been on a subway or any other type of train since I was a teenager. I stop in my tracks and the person behind me bumps into me.

"Come on lady, move out of the way," says a man and he disappears down the stairs. My legs don't move. I stand there, watching people rush down the stairs. I look to my right, and people are all around, waiting for the parade that isn't going to start for at least a couple more hours. I can tell people are annoyed that I am slowing their pace to get to the stairway, but I can't move. I can feel tears clinging to my cheeks.

"Are you all right? Do you need help down the stairs?" It's a young woman, and she has taken my arm. She reminds me of Twiggy, big eyes and a pixie cut. I can't help but stare at her, she looks like so many nameless faces I had seen many years ago. "Are you all right?" she asks.

"I don't think I can go down there," I say. I look at her, and she, along with everything else turns to black and white. There is no noise, just people slowly walking down the stairs. There are people standing at the sidewalks but they aren't waiting for a parade. They're watching people walk by, slowly, with solemn faces. Men, women, children walking down the street. They are wearing winter coats with a yellow star on the lapel, they are carrying a small suitcase, possessions they can't live without. *Walk faster! What are you looking at – eyes front. Do you want to be shot right here in the street?*

"Can I help you get somewhere?" asks the girl.

"I think I want to go home," I whisper.

"Do you live nearby?" she asks.

"A few blocks, down there, but I'm supposed to go to my daughter's. She's waiting."

"I can help you, either go down those stairs or back to your home," she says with a smile.

"I want to go home, but I'm sure you have better things to do," I say.

"I'm just waiting for my boyfriend. We're going to watch the parade. I'll walk with you, I really don't mind," she says with a smile. She takes my arm and we turn to head in the other direction, towards home.

"Thank you," I say, and we walk towards the penthouse. With every step it seems more and more people crowd the sidewalk, and so do security. Up ahead are police officers. Their navy blue uniforms turn into dark olive; their faces turn to stone, their eyes narrow, looking right at me. I could feel myself cower, despising them, despising myself for feeling this way. I promised myself long ago I would never let myself feel that way again – so small, so scared, so inferior. I have never been so relieved to see my building in all the years I've lived here.

"Mrs. McNamara, back so soon?" asks George. "And you are…" he says to the girl.

"I'm Gretchen. She needed some help, so I walked her back here."

"I'm sorry, did you say Greta?" I ask.

"No ma'am, Gretchen," she says.

"I'm sorry, I could have sworn …" I whisper.

"Are you all right Mrs. McNamara?" asks George. He exchanges looks with Gretchen.

"I'll be fine, George, I'm not feeling very well. I want to go upstairs."

"Of course, right away," says George. He comes from behind his desk to assist me.

"Gretchen, thank you so much. Happy Thanksgiving, dear," I say as I shake her gloved hand.

"You too, get some rest, okay? Oh, and you better call your

daughter," says Gretchen. She gives my hand a soft squeeze. "Yes, I'll call her," I promise. "Thanks again, you're very sweet to help an old woman." "Don't be silly," says Gretchen. "Take care." She walks out of the lobby, into the sun. "You're sure you'll be all right, ma'am?" asks George. We walk over to the elevator and he presses the button for me.

"I'll be fine, I'm going to go rest," I say as I enter the elevator alone.

"Please call down if you need anything," says George.

"You're a good man, George. You go enjoy your dry turkey." George lets out a genuine laugh as the elevator doors close. I am alone and I begin to cry.

2

Olivia

"Mom, did you hear the doorbell?" asks Alex, not looking up from his video game.

"I did, did you? Perhaps you could pause your video game and answer it." I can't help but roll my eyes, sometimes these kids can be so ... lazy. I hate to use that word because they really aren't, but it seems like when I need them to click in, they don't. "You kids need to help out today, okay? I've got a lot going on in the kitchen."

"What do you mean, 'you kids'?" says Abbie. "I've been helping you all day."

"Yes, you have, but please, don't stop now. The day's not over yet. I need to conserve my strength for – "

"Okay, let's just put a smile on our faces and answer the door," says Tim walking in from the kitchen towards the front door. "Tis the season, right?"

"You're so cute," I say and give his cheek a squeeze.

Tim opens the door and there stands Uncle Charlie and Aunt Phyllis. "Happy Thanksgiving, come on in." He gives Aunt Phyllis a kiss on her cheek and shakes Uncle Charlie's hand. "How was the drive?"

"Fine, fine," says Uncle Charlie. "Smells great in here."

"The table looks beautiful, Olivia," says Aunt Phyllis.

"Oh, thank you. Can I get you some tea?"

"No tea, but I'd love a glass of wine. Where's your mother?" asks Aunt Phyllis, looking around.

"She'll be here, don't worry." I don't have the strength for this woman. She doesn't even wait five minutes before she is looking around, taking inventory, looking for something to insult or pick at. I promised Tim I would be on my best behavior since today is Thanksgiving, but on the inside I am waiting for Mother to arrive. She always knows how to politely put Phyllis in her place. I feel bad for Uncle Charlie. I don't know how he stands it day in and day out.

"Why didn't she stay over last night like she usually does?" asks Aunt Phyllis. She goes over to the sliding glass door and looks out the window, sipping her wine.

"I'm not sure, I guess things are a little different this year," I walk into the kitchen. I can feel myself getting angry and I don't want to be pushed by this woman again, not today. I wish Mother would get here.

"Grandma's sad," says Abbie. "She didn't want to stay here without Grandpa."

"That's nonsense," says Aunt Phyllis. "She should be around her family."

"It's not nonsense. It's how she *feels*," says Abbie. My outspoken daughter. I don't know whether to be proud or embarrassed.

Tim walks into the living room. "All right, what's going on in here?" he asks, looking at Aunt Phyllis, then Abbie. "You okay sweetie?"

"Yep, fine. I'm going to help Mom in the kitchen."

"Perhaps, Aunt Phyllis, this one time, you could keep your opinions to yourself? Think of it as a favor to your favorite nephew," says Tim, and kisses her cheek.

"What's wrong with everyone? Elizabeth won't stay here without William? Olivia huffs off into the kitchen? Now Abbie does the same? He's gone, Tim. I'm sorry to say it, but he's not coming back."

"Well, that lasted all of what, ten seconds? We all know he's not coming back. Did it occur to you at all that this is the first major holiday without him? That he is missed? Cross your mind at all?"

"Well, no, I guess it didn't. I apologize," says Phyllis and takes a sip of wine.

"I'm not the one you need to apologize to," says Tim.

7

In true Aunt Phyllis fashion, she simply rolls her eyes and takes another sip of wine.

"You may want to ease up on that as well," said Tim. "Tends to make you a little cranky."

"Why, I nev-"

"Oh yes you have, and now it's time for you to behave," says Tim, and he walks into the kitchen. Abbie is at the kitchen table, folding some linen napkins for the table.

I pick up the phone and dial Mother's number. After two rings the machine comes on the line. "Hi, Mom, it's me. Wondering where you are. Hope everything is okay." I start to whisper into the phone, "Mom, please don't leave me here alone with Aunt Phyllis, I don't have the energy. She's in rare form today, and she's already hit the wine."

"Hey –" says Tim, chuckling.

I hang up the phone. "I left another message."

"So I heard," smiles Tim and pulls me into a hug. "Don't worry, I won't leave you alone with the *evil one*."

"Maybe I should go into the city and get her."

"You're not going to be able to get anywhere near there, you know that. It was just on the news the subway is down and to expect delays."

"Maybe Aunt Phyllis could ride her broomstick into the city," says Abbie.

"Good Lord, Abbie. *Please* don't start ..." I can't get overly mad at Abbie, she's my mini. I hope Aunt Phyllis can't hear what she says. When the witch leaves, anything is fair game.

I turn when I hear the swinging kitchen door open. "What's going on in here," says Aunt Phyllis. Her arms are crossed and she looks annoyed.

"Nothing, I tried to reach Mother again. I left her a message."

"Well, maybe she's on her way, then. I hope she's not too long, that turkey is going to be freezing cold if we wait much longer. Such a shame, it looks delicious, too."

"Don't worry, Aunt Phyllis, we will be eating soon enough," says Tim.

"I would like to have a nice dinner, that's all. Not all this drama," says Aunt Phyllis, and before anyone has time to respond, she walks back into the dining room to Uncle Charlie. "I guess we're going to have a cold dinner, Charlie," we hear her say.

"See? Broomstick wasn't all that far off, right?" Abbie says with a smirk.

"We should start dinner," says Tim. "Maybe she'll show up in a little while." He gives me a kiss and walks out of the kitchen. Abbie follows Tim into the dining room.

I pick up the phone, but this time I dial a different number, and sure enough, after one ring there is an answer.

"George, this is Olivia, Elizabeth McNamara's daughter. We were expecting her here for dinner, and she hasn't arrived yet. Have you seen her today?"

"Happy Thanksgiving, Olivia. She left earlier but then she came back. She said she wasn't feeling well. She was actually with someone when she returned."

"She was? Who was it?" I wasn't expecting this news.

"A girl in her mid-twenties, I'd guess. Her name is Gretchen."

"But she seemed okay? Did she look like she was sick?"

"Well, she looked a little agitated, a little pale. She said she wanted to rest."

"I see, well, thank you George. I was starting to get worried, I didn't know who else to call."

"Don't give it a second thought. Try to have a nice holiday," says George.

I walk into the dining room. "I just spoke to George, and apparently Mother isn't feeling well. She wanted to rest."

"Who is *George*," says Aunt Phyllis.

"He works in Grandma's building," says Abbie.

"You called the *doorman* Olivia?"

I take a deep breath and look at her, right in the eyes. "Yes, I did. Is there something wrong with that?"

"No, no, of course not," says Aunt Phyllis, a little rattled at the confrontation.

I give Tim my 'never again' look and don't wait for a response. He knows what I am thinking. "Alex, more turkey?"

"Sure, mom. Dad, we're watching the game later, right?"

"What time does it start?" asks Uncle Charlie. "I don't want to miss it."

"We'll be on the road by then," says Aunt Phyllis. "No time for that foolishness."

Tim and Uncle Charlie exchange a look. "I suppose not," he says. "I guess I'll catch the highlights during the news."

"It starts soon, right?" asks Abbie, with a big smile on her face. She picks up her empty plates and takes it into the kitchen.

"Abbie, *really*," I can't believe my daughter. She is something else, and I couldn't be more proud of her.

3

Tim

I'm watching her from the kitchen doorway as she stares out the window, slowly washing a dish, mesmerized by her own thoughts. "Anything interesting out there?" I ask.

The dish drops into the sink. "Tim, you startled me."

"Sorry. You were in deep thought. Want to talk about it?"

"I was prepared for one parent not to be here today, not both," says Olivia. Another dish is placed into the drying rack.

"I'm sorry about Aunt Phyllis. I know she's impossible," I say.

"I'm used to her by now, don't worry about it. I expected no less from her." Olivia goes back to washing the dishes.

"I know you're worried about your mother, but I'm sure she's fine."

"I know. She just seems so ... vulnerable? I'm not sure how to explain it. It's been a long day I think I need some rest too. I'm going to go see her tomorrow before I bring Abbie to Jessie's house for their sleepover. They want to work on a history project together this weekend."

"Want some help with the dishes?" I ask.

"No thanks, I'm done actually. I think I'll just head upstairs."

"I'm pretty tired myself," I say with a yawn. I'm not used to seeing my wife this way, agitated and exhausted at the same time.

"Are you coming to bed?" asks Olivia as she turns the lights off in the kitchen and heads towards the staircase.

"I just want to watch a little news. I'll be up in a bit." I can't help but watch her. 'Liv'?"

She turns around, halfway up the stairs. "Yeah?"

"She's going to be all right, you know. We all are."

11

Olivia half-smiles and nods. "Don't stay up too late," she says and continues up the stairs. I watch her long hair sway as her slender body moves. High school sweethearts, twenty-plus years and two kids later, and she still moves me like no one else can.

4

Abbie

The elevator in Grandma's building is like no other. Red carpet, mirrored walls, soft music playing in the background. If you didn't watch the numbers change you'd never know you were moving – it doesn't make a sound. It's also quite large, large enough for my mother to pace back and forth.

"Shouldn't we have called first? Grandma isn't really a 'drop-in' kind of person," I ask.

"Don't worry, she won't mind. It's just us."

"If she's sick, maybe we should leave her alone," I say, hoping to convince my mother this is a bad idea. "Or just call her from the car or something."

"Nonsense, we're going to make sure she's all right and then I'll get you to Jessie's by –"

"Eleven, Mom. I told her I'd be there at eleven." Something tells me I'm going to be late. I hate being late. I get that from Grandpa, or so I'm told.

"Yes, I know. Eleven."

The elevator door opens to a bright white hallway with a wooden round table in the center of the hall. A large silk flower arrangement brightens the area. Grandma is the only one on this floor, and everything she touches somehow becomes beautiful, even a hallway.

I knock on the door and wait a few moments. "She must be sleeping, let's *go*."

"She probably didn't hear that, I barely heard it," my mother says. She bangs on the door much louder. I'm glad there's no one else on this floor, or I'd be so embarrassed.

"Coming … I'm *coming*," I can hear from inside. It's Grandma and she doesn't sound like herself.

"*See*, we woke her."

"She was probably in her room, Abbie. Don't be so uptight." Mom stares at the door like she's on a mission or something.

"I'm not uptight, I'm … *respectful*," I say.

The door opens and Grandma is almost unrecognizable. Her long salt-and-pepper hair hangs uncombed, and she looks tiny, tying her pale pink silky robe.

"Come on in you two. I'm sorry," she says, trying to arrange her hair with her fingers. "I must be a sight. I just woke up."

"It's almost nine thirty, you're usually up at the crack of dawn," says Mom.

"I was up earlier, Olivia, but I went back to bed. Abbie, do you have a game today?"

"Not today. I'm on my way to my friend Jessie's house. We're working on a history project."

"Oh, what do you have to do for that?"

"We have to watch this movie and write a report about it," I tell her and place a DVD in Grandma's hands.

"*Schindler's List*," she says. The weirdest look appears on her face, an expression I've never seen her make before.

"Have you seen it?" I ask.

"No," she says as she turns and walks in to the kitchen.

"Grandma? Where are you going?" *Why is she acting so different all of a sudden?*

"I'm making some tea, would you like some?"

"Sure," says my mother.

"We actually have to go soon," I say. "Mom, you *promised*. Eleven, remember?"

"Just a quick cup," says mom. "I'll make it quick, don't worry.

I throw myself into a chair and glare at my mother, but put on a smile when Grandma returns to the dining room, carrying a tray with the tea on it. "I have some pastries, they're quite delicious. Abbie, help yourself."

"Thanks," I say and take one. "Mmmmm, they *are* good. Try one, Mom."

"I think I will," says Olivia with a wink.

"Grandma, are you feeling better?"

"Sure, sweetie. Better put this back in your bag, so you don't forget it." She puts the DVD next to my dish, face down.

"It's supposed to be … intense. Mom had to sign a permission slip for me to watch it." "We'll probably watch it when she brings it back home," says Mom.

"You'll have to let me know what you think of it," says Grandma. "It's just about ten-thirty, girls. You don't want to be late, right?"

Mom looks at Grandma. She doesn't say anything but she's watching her as though she's studying her. I've never seen Grandma act this way, and by the looks of it, Mom hasn't either.

"Thanks for the snack, Grandma. I hope you feel better," I say and kiss her cheek.

"I will talk to you soon, my sweetheart," she says. "Olivia, I'll talk to you later."

"Of course, Mother. Please get some rest. Call if you need anything."

"Love you both, very much," she says as she closes the door. We're now in the hallway.

"Were we just kicked out of there?" asks Mom.

"No, she knows I have to be somewhere," I say. She nods but I can tell she doesn't agree.

Mom is standing on the opposite side of the elevator, watching the numbers change. She is quiet, deep in thought.

"I miss Grandpa," I say, hoping to ease the tension. "I miss his silly jokes, going with him to Central Park. I miss him reading to me, and kicking around a soccer ball."

"I miss him too," she says as she keeps staring at the changing floor numbers

5

Elizabeth

Clear as day I see your big brown eyes; your dark, wavy hair that reaches your waist. You are smiling, warmth radiating around you. We are running in a field, singing and laughing, just enjoying each other's company. We have no worries, we have each other. In the field, we run and skip and laugh. After a while we collapse in the tall grass and look up into the sky. We create images out of the clouds. A cat, a dog, a rabbit. We talk about what it would be like to be able to fly, and if we ever could how we would fly right up to the clouds and touch them.

We share all of our dreams, our thoughts, and our fears. We promise we will always be there for each other. One day, we will both meet the men of our dreams. We will have a double wedding, and have babies at the same time, both girls, and they would be best friends too.

We do each other's hair, talk about our friends at school, and how neither of us are very good at math. We talk about places we want to go when we are older, maybe even to America. We talk about what America must be like and how exciting it would be to go there, to the envy of all our friends.

You are standing there in your most beautiful pink ruffled dress and your hair in ribbons, waving to me.

One day you were with me, and the next you were gone.

6

Tim

A tiger lily centerpiece, two orange candlesticks burning, the scents of garlic bread and homemade manicotti fill the room. The only sound to be heard are the musical clinks of silverware, brief moans of satisfied taste buds, and a random throat clear. There's nothing like a family dinner, and my wife could be a professional chef if she had the desire to. I'm happy she doesn't.

"Did you finish your history project, Abbie?" I ask.

"Yeah, we finished. You guys *have* to watch the movie. It was *so sad*. I can't even believe that happened to people. We should all watch it after dinner. You too, Grandma."

"I have an early morning appointment, I can't stay too long," says Elizabeth.

Suddenly the room becomes silent. "What appointment, Mother?" asks Olivia.

"I'm having the carpets cleaned, it's been a while," she says.

"You're carpets are perfect, why are you having them cleaned?" my wife seems annoyed.

"They're perfect because I get them cleaned, Olivia. How about dessert, I brought a lovely cheesecake."

"Great," said Olivia. "I wondered what was in that box."

Something is going on between my wife and my mother-in-law.

"Grandma, there's this thing at school next week. Our class is having History Week, and on Friday there are some people coming, people who were at the Holocaust. You know, the camps. Will you come with us?"

She drops her fork and coughs. "The camps – you mean survivors? People go around talking about that?" She looks horrified. A typical family dinner has turned into one of the

17

strangest experiences I've ever had.

"I guess so, my teacher said it's a once in a lifetime opportunity," says Abbie. "Will you come?"

"Mother? You look flush. Tim, will you open the window? It's warm in here."

"Sure, be right back," I say.

"Grandma, will you?" asks Abbie. I give her a "now is not the time to push" look.

"Yes, sweetheart. Yes, of course," says Elizabeth. "Don't make a fuss. I think maybe I should get home."

"I'll get your coat," I say, and leave the room to get it.

"Abbie, come give your Grandma a hug," says Elizabeth.

"Did I upset you Grandma? I'm sorry if I did," asks Abbie.

"No, my angel. You are just the way your mother was at your age," says Elizabeth.

"See you on Friday?" asks Abbie.

"I'll see you on Friday," says Elizabeth, and gives Abbie a warm embrace.

About an hour later, Olivia returns home. She smiles when she sees I have cleaned up not only the living room but the kitchen.

"Did you hit some traffic?" I ask.

"That ride home was longer than usual, at least it seemed that way. She stared out the window and talked about the city being so beautiful at night. I don't know what's going on with her."

"Did you ask her?" I ask, pulling her into my arms. She looks frustrated and tired and in dire need of a hug.

"I asked her if something was wrong, she would tell me, right? She insisted there is nothing to tell and started talking about the stupid lights again."

"I agree she has been a little 'off' lately, but maybe it's nothing more than missing your father. Maybe – and don't get angry at me for saying this – but maybe you should ease up a little bit, let her come around in her own time." I take a step back in anticipation of getting punched in the arm.

"Yeah, maybe you're right," she says.

"What was that?" I ask.

"Maybe you were right," she says again, looking down at the floor.

"How'd that taste coming out of your mouth," I tease.

"Like vinegar," she says. And there it is, that beautiful laugh.

7

Elizabeth

It's Friday afternoon and the drive to Olivia's is beautiful. The light snow that arrived through the night sparkles in the sun. Abbie's chatter fills the car, her laughter contagious. I think of myself at that age, how things were so different. Abbie has a childhood surrounded by her family, a lovely home, good friends, and freedom. Every child deserves those things and even though I didn't have those things myself, my heart allows me to be happy for those who are more fortunate. I remember the childhood I had before I was twelve, and the joy and happiness of those years fulfill me to this day.

Pulling into the driveway I see Tim and Alex engaged in a friendly snowball fight.

"Shouldn't you two be shoveling?" asks Olivia, smiling.

"Taking a little break, honey," says Tim. "Your son is ruthless."

"*My* son?"

"Hi Grandma," says Alex.

"Where is my hug, young man?"

"I'm all wet, I'll get you inside." The boys take the grocery bags out of the car and into the house. Olivia's house is 'lived in' but lovely. Everything has its place and there is just enough decoration to provide comfort without clutter. I enjoy my time here but I'm not ready to give up the penthouse.

We have homemade pizza and salad for dinner. Quick and easy, perfect for a night like tonight. We have to be at Abbie's school at 6:30. There was no way for me to get out of going to this event with the family. To tell them I was sick would bring needless worry. Somehow I will get through this night.

8

Olivia

We walk into the auditorium and find our seats. Mother insists on an aisle seat in case she needs to get up for some reason. I can tell she still is not feeling well, but as usual, she never complains.

I put my hand on her shoulder, and she turns to give me her loving smile. "You okay?" I ask her.

"Not sure what to expect." I see her start to look around the room. She looks anxious and nervous.

"What a nice room. I wonder how many people it can hold. Those curtains, on the stage, what a lovely color of burgundy. I wonder where she got that sweater, how nice," says Mother. Her thoughts are all over the place, so unlike her.

"Mother, what are you doing?" I ask. I take her hand and give it a squeeze. I don't know why, it's something I've done as long as I can remember.

"I'm looking around," she says, as if I'm asking an inappropriate question.

"You've been in this 'lovely room,' which is a gymnasium by the way, a hundred times. And that sweater is *hideous*."

"Not *that* sweater, that one in front of her, the dark green one."

"Oh. Well that one's okay I guess." We share a chuckle. "You look a little flush, Mother. Would you like to use the restroom, maybe splash some water on your face? I'll go with you if you'd like."

"No, I'm fine," she says. Doesn't she know I can tell she isn't?

Abbie returns to her seat holding some papers. "Here you go, Grandma. Here, Mom."

"What's this?" I ask, taking the folded light blue paper.

"A program. See the cover? Our class designed it."

"I love the cover, nice job," I say. I open the program, and start to read through it. There are a few advertisements from local companies who sponsored History Week, a couple of notes of thanks to staff members, and then there was a note of thanks to the night's speakers.

> Oskar Rosenthaal
> Rachel Weissman
> Malka Prinz-Howard
> Nikolais Joachim
> Isaak Liebowitz

Mother opens her program and starts reading it as well. I hear her gasp, she has seen something, but what on earth in the program could upset her? I scan through the program, and I don't know what she's reacting to. I start to ask her what the matter is but then a man walks onto the stage.

"Good evening, everyone, I'm Rodney Allan, head of the History Department. I hope you had a chance to see the various pieces of artwork, reports, and photos that line the halls leading into this room. These were all created by our students, your children. I hope you are as proud of what they've done as I am. We have had a great week and I am excited that after a lot of phone calls, scheduling, making reservations and arrangements, that we are able to end History Week with this amazing night. Many of you know the story of the Holocaust, and tonight we will be hearing from Holocaust survivors. As you know, there weren't that many, and there are certainly fewer now, so please help me welcome our speakers."

All of a sudden Mother stands up, and her purse falls to the floor. I hear everything spill out.

"Mother, what is it?" I ask her in a whisper.

"Grandma?" Abbie whispers.

Her eyes close and she collapses to the ground. "Tim, call 911!"

9

Olivia

She looks so tiny in the hospital bed. Her salt and pepper hair surrounds her head like a halo on the pillow, flowing off to the side. When I was little, I would brush her hair and give her pigtails. "Beauty parlor," we would call it. Then she would do my hair and we would model for Daddy.

The steady, annoying beeps from the machines bring me back to my reality. A heart attack, the doctor told us. My mother had a heart attack. Nurses come in and out, making sure everything is just right. Sitting here with her, looking at her, listening to the machines, watching her breathe; these are moments I will never forget.

I feel a little tap on my arm. I jump because I didn't hear anybody enter the room. "If I could get in there," says Jackie, the nurse. "I need to flush the IV line."

"Of course," I say and stand at the foot of the bed. She pulls up the sleeve of the johnny, which even though it is the smallest adult size they have, it is still too big for Mother, and she begins to flush the IV line. I can't help but notice something dark on her arm. I have never seen it before. I move closer, to the left side of the bed. "What is that?" It's hard to tell, because some of the tubing tape is covering part of it.

Jackie lifts Mother's arm so we can both get a closer look. "You've never seen this?" she asks, looking a little uncomfortable.

"No," I say. "Do you know what it is?"

"Looks like your mother has survived much more than a heart attack," says Jackie.

I look at her, confused. I have no idea what Jackie is talking about, and Jackie looks like she knows the answer but doesn't want to say.

"Well, um, I'm not sure … but it looks like a tattoo," says Jackie. "A tattoo, from World War Two, maybe."

"A *tattoo*? From the war? You mean like from a concentration camp?" This makes no sense. She's not even Jewish, she's Catholic! "She would have told me about something like this. Right?"

"I … I don't know," stutters Jackie. "I need to check on my other patients, but if you need me to, I can stay a few more minutes."

"No, that's okay. You go ahead." Jackie leaves the room and I go to the other side of the bed to get a closer look. Thoughts fill my head – *Who are you? What have you been through? Why have you never told me?* I look at her arm closely, her soft pale skin interrupted by faded dark ink. The IV bandages prevent me from seeing the entire number. *How did I never see this?*

"Thought you could use some coffee," says Tim as he enters the hospital room. He stops short when he sees Olivia. She is sitting beside the bed, her head buried into her mother's arm, crying hysterically.

"Hey, what is it?" he asks. He puts the coffee down on the counter.

"I don't know her at all. I thought I knew everything about her," she says between sobs.

"Sweetie, you're not making any sense. Take a breath, and tell me what's going on."

"Look at her arm," she says, sobbing.

Tim pulls back the johnny. He looks, then closes his eyes for a moment, understanding.

"I've never seen that before. *Ever.* She has never said a word about it. All these years, how did I never *see* that?" Olivia continues to bury her head in her left arm, the right hand still holding her mother's hand.

"I don't know – I don't know what to say. When she's up to it you will ask her, but not right now," says Tim. How do you handle a moment like this?

"She's got some explaining to do, that's for sure," says Olivia, wiping her face.

"Liv, she's had a heart attack, you're going to have to go easy on her," says Tim.

Just then, Abbie enters the room. "Dad, the vending machine isn't working, can I have another dollar?"

"Not now, Abbie," says Tim, not even turning to look at her.

"Why's mom crying? Did something else happen to Grandma?" asks Abbie. She takes a step forward to see what's going on.

Tim stands and leads Abbie out of the room. "Come on, Abbie. We'll fix the vending machine."

"Wait, what's wrong with mom?" asks Abbie, trying to look around Tim to see her mother. "Dad, wait, I don't want to go. What's going on here? What's up with Mom?"

"She's fine honey. She's worried about Grandma."

"Well, so am I but I'm not balling my eyes out. Seriously, I'm not a little kid, you can tell me stuff."

"Apparently, this family is full of secrets," says Olivia.

"What's *that* supposed to mean?" asks Abbie.

"Let's go," says Tim and takes Abbie's arm to lead her out of the room.

"You and my daughter are going to be the death of me, I swear," whispers Olivia, taking her mother's hand. The tears continue to fall as Olivia gazes out the window. She strokes her mother's hand tenderly. So many years of secrets, so many questions.

10

Elizabeth

I can feel my body but I can't open my eyes. I feel so …
heavy. I can hear a faint beeping and suction sound. There are
voices, both male and female, but I only hear fragments,
"surgery went well" "… more tests" "…lucky she got here when
she did".

Again, I try to open my eyes. They won't open. I hear a
man's voice. One more try – *yes!* Everything is blurry. I turn
my head towards the voices. *Everything is so sore.* I try to lift
my hand, but it doesn't move.

"Ouch! Stop stepping on my feet!" We are all close together,
swaying with the cattle car. It is dark, except for small, rhythmic
flashes of light through the cracks in the wooden walls. I am
pressed against my mother, who is holding my brother. My
sister is right beside me. There is a bucket in the corner, but I
cannot make it over there, it is too crowded. I don't know what
to do, I cannot hold it any longer. I feel the warmth run down
my leg, I am so embarrassed. I look at my sister. "It's okay,"
she says. "I had to do it, too." My humiliation has gotten the
best of me, and I start to cry. "Sister, don't worry. When we get
to our new home, we will bathe." She puts her arm around me,
always the strong one. With her by my side, everything will be
okay … I hope.

"There she is. Welcome back, Mrs. McNamara," a tall man
in a white physician's coat says. "I'm Dr. Krane. You gave your
family quite a scare, but you're going to be fine. Jackie, why
don't you get her some ice chips."

"Yes, doctor," a female voice says.

"Let's raise your bed a little bit," says Dr. Krane. He has
what I call 'doctor eyes' and that is very comforting to me. He

has a sparkle in his eye that says he knows what he is doing but at the same time cares about you. I know that he is going to take good care of me. I look around the room; there are so many machines, and wires, and people coming in and out of the room. I was hoping to see Olivia, but she must be waiting somewhere.

"Where is my family?"

"They're in the waiting room. Don't worry, you'll see them soon. You've just come up from Recovery a little while ago. Jackie will take your vitals now," says Dr. Krane.

"I don't remember anything, what happened to me?"

"You are very fortunate your family got you here when they did. You had a heart attack, Mrs. McNamara. I performed a procedure called a coronary angioplasty not long after you arrived."

"A what?"

"A coronary angioplasty. You had some arteries that were blocked; I opened them so the blood will flow more freely to your heart. I inserted a catheter that was equipped with a balloon which is inflated to open the blocked artery. Simultaneously, a metal mesh stent was inserted into the artery to keep it open long term."

"I think I understand what you're saying, but in layman terms, am I going to be okay?"

"You are on the road to recovery, and it's a process. The fact that you're active and you take good care of yourself is going to be helpful. You will need to have patience with yourself and with us. You're going to be here awhile, and from here you will start cardiac rehabilitation. For now, we're going to keep a very close eye on you. We'll take it one step at a time. You're at the beginning of the journey. Do you have any questions?"

"No, not right now. I think I'll let what you told me … absorb."

"I know, it's a lot of information thrown at you all at once. Are you comfortable? What would you say your pain level is right now, on a scale of one to ten, ten being the most severe."

"Three or four, I guess. I feel numb and heavy all over."

"Your body has been through a lot. Are you up for some visitors?"

"Of course. They must be so worried," I say, a little worried myself.

"I just updated them. They're glad you're okay," says Dr. Krane and starts to leave the room.

"Dr. Krane?"

"Yes?" he says, turning around.

"Thank you. Thank you for saving my life today."

"My part was easy. You have the hard part – you have a lot of work to do now," he says. "But you're welcome all the same," and he leaves the room.

A few moments later, Olivia, Tim and the kids rush into the room.

"Grandma!" Abbie rushes to my side and collapses on top of me.

"Oh!" I gasp.

"Abbie, be careful!" says Tim, pulling her back.

"I'm so sorry, Grandma. I … I was so worried about you."

"I know, but you must be careful, okay?" I smile at her, my sweet girl.

"I will. Sorry." She steps aside and Alex steps towards me.

"Alex, my boy, I'm so happy to see you." I look at his NYU t-shirt and smile. He worked so hard to get into that school. "My handsome boy, give Grandma a kiss."

Alex leans over and kisses my forehead. He feels so warm. "How do you feel? You know, besides being crushed by Abbie and all."

"Be quiet, Alex," pouts Abbie.

"Sore, and tired. And very happy to see my family. Olivia, why are you way over there?" Olivia is standing near the doorway, and doesn't say a word, but moves aside when Dr. Krane enters the room.

"Dr. Krane, what happens now, how long will she be here?" asks Olivia.

"As I told your mother, this is a process. She'll be here for a while, and then she will start cardiac rehabilitation. She will have a long road of rest, tests, more rest and more tests. It's important to focus on the recovery, not the clock or the calendar."

"I see," says Olivia, and crosses her arms.

Why won't she even look at me? She must be worried. She has always worried about everything too much.

"I'll be back to check on you later," says Dr. Krane.

"Thank you. And if I'm going to be here a while, you need to call me something other than 'Mrs. McNamara'."

"You're the boss," he smiles, and leaves the room. We are all together, happy with Dr. Krane's good news. Abbie is chattering about an upcoming game, Alex about his classes.

All of a sudden we hear a knock at the door. We all look at each other because everyone who is supposed to be here is here already.

Tim opens the door and goes out in the hall to speak to someone. "Hi, can I help you?" he asks. It is an older woman, wearing a dark overcoat, a dark hat and a beautiful floral scarf. She has striking features and a warm smile.

"Hello," she says. "I was there, at the school. I was one of the speakers. Mr. Allan told me she was here, and I was wondering if she's okay."

"Wow, that's really kind of you to come check on her. She had a heart attack, but she's going to be fine after some time and rehab. They're only letting family in the room right now, but I'll tell her you came by. What's your name?"

"My name is Malka. Malka Prinz-Howard."

"Thank you, Malka, for coming. That was really nice of you."

"I am in town for a few more days, maybe I'll come back again before I leave the city."

"Maybe by then she'll be able to see you," says Tim. "Well, I better get back in there. Thanks again for coming."

"I will say a prayer for your … mother?"

"Mother-in-law. Her name is Elizabeth."

"How nice. I will pray for Elizabeth. Good night," says Malka, and she turns to head towards the elevator down the hall.

"I'm sorry we didn't get to hear your story. That's a wonderful thing you do, educating people, especially the students." He looks at her and he can tell she is a kind woman. Her eyes sparkle in the soft lighting of the hallway.

"That's very kind of you to say, thank you," says Malka, as she puts her gloves on.

"Well, goodnight then," says Tim. "That was interesting," he says as he walks back into the room.

"What do you mean? Who was that?" asks Olivia.

"You're not going to believe this," says Tim. "She was one of the speakers at the school." Turning to me, he says "She came to see if you were all right."

"That was nice of her," says Olivia. "How did she know Mother was here?"

"Mr. Allan told her," says Tim.

"Did you ask her what her name was?" I ask. I couldn't imagine who would have come here.

"Of course. She said she was going to be in town for a few more days and may come back to see if you can have regular visitors."

"And her name was …" says Alex, being his impatient self.

"It was different. Malka?"

"Malka?" *She was here!* My heart begins beating fast, and I am gasping for air. I want to tell him to go get her, but I'm having trouble breathing and cannot say the words.

An alarm goes off, and Jackie rushes in. "Everyone, please step out of the room so we can tend to her."

"Oh my God," says Olivia. "What's happening?"

"Please, wait outside, I'll be with you as soon as I can," says Dr. Krane. "All right, Elizabeth. We're here."

The door closes, and Olivia starts to pace the hallway. "I can't believe this. I can't believe *any* of this!"

"She'll be okay, Mom," says Abbie. "It's Grandma."

"Come sit with us, Mom," says Alex.

"I'll sit with you," says Tim. "Mom needs to pace right now."

It seems like hours before Dr. Krane comes out of the room. "We've had a little set-back, but she's comfortable now. No more visiting tonight. You can come back tomorrow, but she's sleeping now."

"Dr. Krane, can't I say goodnight to her?" asks Olivia.

"She's already asleep, I don't want her disturbed," says Dr. Krane.

"Come on, Olivia. You heard him, she's sleeping. We all need to rest, too," says Tim.

"I just want to see her, see that she's okay," says Olivia.

"Look at her through the window," says Tim. Olivia walks over to the window of the room. She puts her hand on it but doesn't say anything.

"Mom, let's go. We should go now," says Abbie, tugging on her sleeve.

"I suppose. Okay, but we'll be back in the morning," says Olivia.

11

Elizabeth

It's day four in the hospital, and even before I open my eyes I can sense there is someone in my room with me. I lay there with my eyes closed, still tired, waiting for them to say something. I realize I am holding my breath, and quietly begin to breathe again. I slowly open my eyes, and look to my left. There is an empty chair in the corner, the door to the restroom, slightly ajar, and then a small counter with a small sink and medical supplies on a shelf with cabinets above most likely containing more supplies. I then look to the right, towards the window, and since the sun is shining so brightly, I only see a shadow of a figure.

"Olivia – is that you honey?"

The shadow moves a little closer. "No, I'm not Olivia. I was told you could have visitors, so I came in. I'm sorry, maybe I shouldn't have come. "

"Oh. Well, yes, I'm up to visitors, but could you come over here, out of the sun's glare? I can't see you that well."

She comes to my side, and I can't help but gasp. *It's her.* She is smiling at me. *That smile. Can't you tell it's me?* I touch my cheek, and realize the bandage is still on my face. I was told by Jackie, the nurse, that when I had my heart attack, I collapsed I hit one of the folding chairs and needed some stitches. The bandage is quite large. *She doesn't recognize me yet.*

"How are you feeling?" she asks. "Your son-in-law told me you had a heart attack. I felt so badly, I decided to come and see you before I left town. It's Elizabeth, right?"

"Yes, Elizabeth. Elizabeth McNamara. Thank you for coming to see me."

"I brought these for you, I hope you like them." From behind her back she presents the most beautiful bouquet of flowers. A wonderful mixture of roses, Gerber daisies, carnations, sunflowers and greenery tied together with a silk purple ribbon.

"They are so beautiful, how thoughtful," I say. *You're really here, in this room.* She leans them towards me so I can smell them, and the scent is just exquisite. *Running through the field of wild flowers, do you remember? Do you remember those days? Those were the best days of our lives, my favorite childhood memory.*

"I'm sorry, I'm forgetting myself. I'm Malka –"

"Yes, I know who you are, I can't believe you're here. You're really here! I saw your name in the program, and that's when my heart started racing. After all these years, I can't believe it. The last time I saw your name written was – well, it doesn't matter now."

"I'm sorry," says Malka. She takes a step back, almost cautiously, not knowing what's going on. "Have we met?"

"My name is Elizabeth McNamara," I say.

"Yes, you said – "

"Elizabeth is the name I gave myself when I came to America. McNamara is my married name. Malka, don't you recognize me?"

She tilts her head, curious, and takes a step forward. Her eyes squint, then widen. She lets out a gasp. "Nava? Oh, I knew it. I just knew it!" She is crying, almost sobbing.

What? "What did you know, sister?"

"I knew you were alive. I always thought that I would know it deep in my heart if you had died. I carried the hope with me all these years – that somehow, someday I would see you again."

"Sister," I say and I extend my arms. "Let me hold you, I need to know that this is real."

Malka sits on the bed and we hold each other and just cry and cry and then cry some more. Sixty years of worrying, wondering and praying has brought us to this moment of pure joy. She sits up straight. "Let me look at you, you're so beautiful. You have aged well, sister. Life has been good to you in America?"

"Oh, yes. How about you, have you had a good life as well?" I want to know it all, every detail.

"Oh Nava, I've had an extraordinary life. When the camp was liberated I was so sick, I didn't think I would survive. I met a doctor, Joshua Howard, an American. Well, it didn't take long for us to fall in love. We were married, and we have four beautiful children. I'm even a grandmother! What about you, when did you marry? You changed your name, I guess that's why I couldn't find you."

"You ... looked for me?"

"Of course I looked for you, you're my sister! Years and years we made inquiries, we even hired a private investigator, but he didn't turn up anything. I decided then that I would keep praying and let God bring us together when He was ready."

"I ... I thought you had died. I felt so guilty, Malka. I felt responsible, I just couldn't bear to think about it. I came here when I was healthy enough to travel. I changed my name, I got a job, a room in a boarding house, and then a few years later, I met William, and it was then that I let myself trust someone, love someone, and be taken care of."

"Oh, Nava. Why on earth would you feel guilty?"

"I ... I was such a stupid girl. A very stupid and selfish girl. Can you ever forgive me?" At this moment all the emotions of the past six decades get the best of me, and I just break down sobbing in my sister's arms.

"It's all right, sister. We don't have to talk about it right now. We have the rest of our lives to talk about everything. Oh Nava, everything is just fine now." She holds me and rubs my back with one hand and the back of my head with the other. I am clinging to her, afraid she will vanish if I let go.

12

Tim

I look over to the passenger side of the car. Olivia is in a daze, looking out the window in silence. She has not been the same since she came home from the hospital, and she refuses to talk about it.

"Olivia, please talk to me. What's going on in that beautiful head of yours?"

"I'm fine," she says without looking at me. "I'm worried about Mother, Alex has tests this week, and Abbie wants to do this and that. I'm just a little overwhelmed. With everything."

"Okay, let's take one thing at a time. Dr. Krane is optimistic. Alex is a very smart kid and he studies all the time, so I know he'll do great on his tests. Abbie, is well, Abbie, and she'll be fine too."

"Everything is either black or white with you Tim. It's not always that way," says Olivia.

I realize this conversation is not going to happen while I'm driving, so I pull into a parking lot and turn the car off. "Now, my dearest, we are going to talk."

"I want to get to the hospital, Tim. What are you doing?" she says, wiping tears off her cheek.

"I'm looking at you, and I'm listening. I'm listening, Olivia, so talk to me." I take her hands in my own and start to massage them, as they are trembling. "Just talk. Say whatever you want and I will listen."

She takes a deep breath. "Yesterday, I was sitting in the hospital room with Mother. Jackie, the nurse, came in to flush the IV line, no big deal. But I'm watching her, Jackie, and she pulls up the sleeve to the johnny and does her thing with the IV, but I see something on Mother's arm. It was dark, so I ask Jackie

35

what it is, and I go over to the other side of the bed and we both look at it, it's faded and there is some IV tape over part of it but it's a number or something."

"So again, I ask Jackie what she thinks it is and she says 'It looks like your mother survived more than a heart attack.' And then she asked if I had ever seen it before, and of course I haven't. Jackie thinks it's one of those tattoos, from the war, you know, from the camps. I tell her Mother isn't even Jewish, she's Catholic. Tim, I don't know what to think. I thought I knew everything about her. *Everything.* I don't know *anything.* She's my mother and a stranger all in one body."

"Wow, okay. We can deal with this, Liv. There are a lot of questions, obviously, but Liv, she's had a heart attack, so you've got to go easy on her. She's already had one set-back, she can't take another one. Dr. Krane was firm about that, remember?"

"Yes, I remember," she says. "I just don't understand. How she kept this from me. What about Dad, he must have known, right? He never said a word either. How could she not tell me about her past, and how did I never see that tattoo? I feel so stupid."

I'm not used to seeing her this way, she's always so strong and in control. At this moment she is naked in vulnerability. "You're not stupid, honey. How could you have known, why would you even ask? You need to get some answers, but she needs to be a lot stronger before you ask the questions, don't you agree?"

"Maybe I should talk to Dr. Krane before I see her. Maybe he can tell me how to handle this without creating another set-back."

"That sounds like a plan. Are you ready to go?" She nods and I kiss both of her hands and put them back in her lap. I start the car and wait my turn to blend into the long line of traffic.

"Thank you, Tim. I mean it, you're my rock," she says, and puts her hand on my thigh with a little squeeze.

"Keep doing that and I'll have to pull over again," I say with a grin.

"Tim!" and there it is, that laugh that is music to my ears. The first time I heard that laugh I knew she was going to be my wife and the mother of my children. Since we met in our freshman year of high school I knew I would have to wait many years to marry her, but it was worth it. I would do anything for this woman, anything at all.

13

Olivia

The elevator doors slowly open. A few people step out and go their separate ways. It's just Tim and I there now. "Please," he says. "Please don't upset her. I know you have questions, I know you're upset. Just talk to Dr. Krane before you go in there, okay?"

"I already told you I would, Tim." I look down the hall. "There's Jackie." We walk towards the nurse's station.

"Jackie, hello. Is Dr. Krane in today?"

"He's doing his rounds, Mrs. Roberts. He should be in your mother's room in a little while. Are you all right? You seem upset."

"Well, it's about what you and I … saw yesterday. I want to ask my mother questions about it, but I don't want to upset her."

"I see. I can page Dr. Krane if you'd like."

"That would be great, I appreciate it. How is she this morning, did she sleep well?"

"Your mother is in wonderful spirits this morning. She's had a visitor with her since after breakfast."

"A visitor? Who could that be?" Dismayed, I look at Tim, and he simply shrugs.

"I don't know, but they've been laughing, crying, and hugging for hours now. Whoever it is, she's really happy to see her."

I take Tim's hand. "Let's go in, I want to see who's visiting. Thanks, Jackie. I'll talk to Dr. Krane later."

"Of course, Mrs. Roberts," she says and continues looking at patient charts.

As we approach the room Tim stops in his tracks. "Well, look at that. She came back."

I look up at his profile. "Who?"

"The woman from the other night. It looks like her anyway," he says. "Your mother seems to know her. Maybe we should wait, let them talk."

"What? No way – I want to meet this woman." I head into the room, letting go of his hand. We enter the room and the chatter instantly stops. "Mother?"

"Olivia, Tim. I'm so glad you're here. Come over here, please. I have the most wonderful news."

"Oh?" I look at the woman sitting close to Mother. "I'm Olivia, and you are …"

"That's my news, sweetheart. This is Malka. Malka Prinz-Howard."

"Nice to meet you, Malka. That's a very unique name," I say.

"Not so unique in Czechoslovakia, but thank you," she says with a smile. "Well, it's not known as Czechoslovakia anymore, but it was when we were little girls."

"We?" I ask.

"Olivia, I know this is going to come as a shock to you, but Malka is my sister. My *twin* sister."

I can feel the color leaving my face, and almost feel a little faint. I look at them both, one and then the other and back again. "You don't look like –"

"Fraternal," says Malka. "But twins all the same." They smile at each other, almost giddy like little girls who just told a secret.

"Mother, you've had a heart attack. You also had a set-back a few nights ago, so I don't want to upset you, but I need to know. What the hell is going on here?" I feel myself wanting to cry, to shout, to shake her. "I thought I knew everything about you. *Everything*." I look at Malka. "Do you have one too? A tattoo, do you have one?"

"Olivia," says Mother. "Please calm down. I can explain everything."

"May I see your arm please?" I ask Malka. "Do you have one?"

"Olivia –" pleads Mother. "Don't do this."

"I saw yours yesterday, Mother, when Jackie flushed your IV. How come I've never seen it before? How come you've never told me about it?" She pushes up the sleeve on her johnny and closes her eyes.

Malka rolls up her sleeve. "Yes, Olivia. I have one too, though it's quite faded now." She shows me her arm and looks at me without saying a word. She has a gentle spirit about her, a calming affect one might say. I look back at her. "She never said anything. Mother, how could you never *tell me* about *any* of this? I didn't even know you were Jewish. I thought we were Catholic. Church on Sundays, First Communion, Christmas. We celebrated all those things, remember?"

"Of course I remember, Olivia. Wonderful memories –"

"No, Mother. *Lies.* My whole childhood is a big, fat lie. How could you do that to me?"

"Okay," says Tim. "Everybody needs to take a breath for a minute. Please." He tries to pull me into his arms, but I step forward, towards the end of the bed so I can look at my mother straight on.

"If I could just say something, just for a moment," says Malka. "Olivia, you need to understand something. So many survivors who came to this country … they couldn't talk about their experiences, they were so traumatized, it was just too much. To survive such circumstances, such cruel and inhumane circumstances. To be surrounded by death, seeing the ashes of your family flying out of the chimney day in and day out, sickness, starvation, beatings, torture – to live through all that as teenagers. *Teenagers.* Younger than your own daughter is now. Could you imagine her going through such a thing?"

"No, of course not. I don't know what to think about this. Any of this." I start to pace around the room, trying not to cry. This is all just too much. "I need to go outside and get some fresh air. Tim, come with me."

"Olivia, please stay," I hear Mother say.

"We'll be back in a little while," I say without turning around.

I can't look at her.

"She just needs some fresh air, maybe something to eat," says Tim. "See you in a little while."

Outside in the sun underneath an oak tree, Tim and I sit on a bench. "Tim, how could she keep her past from me?"

"You heard Malka. What she said makes sense, right? What she said about being younger than Abbie, that really put things in perspective didn't it?"

I stop and turn to look at him. I can't believe he is saying these words to me. "Well I'm so glad that everything is so clear to you, that everything is put in the right perspective for you, how nice that is *for you*. I myself need a little more than five minutes to come to grips that my whole life has been a lie! I can feel invisible walls closing in on me, my eyes feel heavy and my cheeks blazing. I look down at my hands, they are trembling. I've never had an anxiety attack, but this must be what one feels like.

"I'm only saying what she said makes sense. I don't want to fight with you, honey. If you could just calm down and listen. Just for a moment. Your mother survived the Holocaust. Think about it, Olivia. More than six million people didn't, but your mother *did*. Let's go back inside and be there for her. She's reunited with her sister after what, sixty years? This is wonderful for her, for our family. I'm just asking you to keep an open mind. *Please*."

I take a few deep breaths. Feeling slightly calmer, I hear myself say, "Okay. Okay, let's go back in."

"That's my girl," says Tim, and takes my hand in his own.

I can't believe I'm going back upstairs. We ride the elevator in silence. I feel badly. Tim tries to make things better, he hates conflict, and he's not used to seeing it between Mother and me. We don't usually fight, ever. But this is more than I can handle right now. I was upset enough that she had a heart attack. *Looks like she's survived more than a heart attack.*

"What are you thinking, Liv?" Tim takes my hand as we leave the elevator.

"I'm trying to imagine her … there. A young girl, with no hair. Having hardly anything to eat, not knowing how long, or even if, she was going to live. Losing her family, or most of it."

"I've got to admit," says Tim. "If I survived that and had a chance to go to another country, I might have done the same thing she did – change my name, try to build a new life for myself, and never speak of it again. That isn't as far-fetched as one might think."

"I don't know, Tim. I don't know what I'd do. I would like to think I would at least share it with my family. She must have told Dad, right? She couldn't possibly keep that from him. They were married over *fifty* years, there's no way he didn't see that tattoo. But then again, she hid it from me all these years. Oh, I just have so many questions."

"And she'll answer them, in time. She's got to focus on her health right now. We can't push her, honey," he says. He pushes my hair back behind my ear. "Hey, don't cry. It's going to be okay, I promise."

"I'm sorry, I can't help it. I just can't get that picture out of my head now. Skinny little bald girl in a striped uniform, God knows all that she saw. How could she hold all that inside? I think I would combust. You know, all Abbie has talked about the past few days is that movie. I wonder how she'll react when she finds out her grandmother is a survivor. And Alex. He will be shocked! He is so protective of her."

"We definitely need to tell them."

"Of course we're telling them. There have been enough secrets."

14

Olivia

Walking towards my mother's room, I realized the door was closed. I peeked through the window blinds and saw Dr. Krane was with her. "Let's just go to the waiting room for a bit, Dr. Krane is in there."

"Sounds good," said Tim. "Maybe there's some coffee in there."

As I round the corner, I see Malka sitting in the waiting room, talking on a cell phone. I motion to Tim to not make a sound so I can hear what she's saying.

"I can't believe it either, sweetheart. So many years, so many prayers, finally answered. I need you to cancel my return ticket. I want to stay here for a while." There is a pause. "Well, I don't know, Isaac. She's going to be in the hospital for who knows how long, I'm not going to leave now, I've just found her." Another pause. "Don't worry son, I'm fine. My hotel is lovely and it's close to the hospital." A long pause. "Maybe when she's stronger the family can come here to visit. I don't think she's up to it now." Short pause. "She's beautiful, Isaac. Just as I remember, except maybe there's a little gray in her hair. There is a large bandage on her face, I didn't even recognize her at first." Another pause. "She hurt her face when she collapsed, but the doctor says she'll be fine."

Malka must have realized someone was nearby, all of a sudden she turned around and caught us eavesdropping. "I'll call you later honey, when I get back to the hotel. Yes, love you too. Bye, bye now."

I take a step forward. "I'm sorry. We were coming in here and then I saw you were on the phone. I'm sorry," I say.

"Not at all, dear, come sit with me. I called my son, Isaac, to let him know the wonderful news. I'm sure he's calling the rest of the family right now."

"How many children do you have, Malka?" asks Tim.

"I have four beautiful children, Isaac is my oldest. He's named after my brother, we just spelled his name with a 'c' instead of a 'k'."

"Brother? There's another sibling I don't know about?" I ask. *How many more secrets are there?*

Malka's expression immediately changes. All of a sudden she looks so ... sad.

"I do not speak of him often, but yes another sibling." She is looking at the floor. "When Nava and I were almost thirteen years old, our mother, after many miscarriages, again became pregnant. When she gave birth to Isaak, my parents were so thrilled, so grateful that God blessed them with a son. He was a beautiful baby, always happy. The only time he cried was when he was hungry, he was such an angel. When we arrived at Auschwitz, we all got off the train. That is when we were separated from our father. Nava and I were in the same line of five as our mother, who was holding Isaak. He must have realized he was hungry, because he began to cry." Malka closed her eyes and put her hand over her mouth.

"You don't have to talk about it if you don't want to," says Tim.

"No, no. I'm okay. It's just been a long time since I've talked about him. My dear, innocent brother. Not even a year old." She wipes her eyes and continues. "He began to cry, and an SS officer came over and told our mother, or rather *screamed* at my mother, to shut that baby up. Of course, that only made Isaak more upset, he wasn't used to screaming of any kind. The SS officer ripped Isaak from my mother's arm and snapped him over his knee. My mother let out a shrill I will never forget. A heartbreaking shrill only a mother could have for her child. The SS officer threw Isaak to the ground, came back to my mother and slapped her hard against her face, almost knocking her to the ground. He threatened to shoot her right there if she didn't stop her wailing."

"Oh my God," says Tim. He squeezes my hand, to keep himself from tearing up I think.

"Somehow she managed to stop her sounds of torment. The line started moving, and another SS officer ahead pointed for my mother to go to the left, and Nava and I were motioned to go to the right. The last vision of my mother is seeing her walk around a corner of a small building. She was walking so slowly. She had been defeated. There was no color in her face, it was if she had just died but somehow was still able to walk."

"I don't know what to say," is all I could say. I too wipe my face as my tears reacting to this story make their way down my neck and chest.

"Your mother and I are twins, but you are right, we are very different. I have always been the strong one, the one with a voice. Your mother, she coped with things by bottling them all up inside. Growing up she was quite shy, unless you were family. It does not surprise me that she came here, changed her name and started a whole new life. That is the Nava I know."

"I've always known her to be quite strong," I say, in her defense.

"Yes, in some ways she's very strong," says Malka. "She is very loyal, she likes to take care of people, and she likes nice things. From what she told me about William, he was perfect for her. He helped her forget her past, and for that I will always be grateful to a man I'll never personally know."

"My father, he was so special," I say. "I miss him every day."

"What if he came back?" asks Malka. "What if for sixty years you thought he was dead and then all of a sudden he came back? How would you feel?"

"He's not coming back," I murmur.

"I know, but what if somehow he did. How would you feel? Excited? Overjoyed?" I nod my head, smiling. "Of course you would," she says.

"Your mother thought I was never coming back, Olivia. Here I am, after all of these years, and we are both in awe that we have been reunited. Your mother confessed something to me this morning. She was afraid that I had died, and she blamed herself for it."

"What? Why would she think that?" I ask. I look up at Tim, he shrugs and waits for Malka's answer.

"Nava worked in Kanada, the warehouse where all the vluables belonging to the prisoners went. Everything was sorted – glasses, jewelry, photos, clothes, shoes, silver – whatever came out of a bag or suitcase, it was all sorted. She became friendly with someone there, Greta. Greta was, shall we say, *involved* with an SS officer. Well, apparently, that officer helped Greta and Nava escape. She asked people to get word to me that she was leaving, but I was never told. I had already been transferred to another camp, and I had asked that people tell her that I was all right, I was just being transferred to another camp and not to worry. She never got my message either. She was riddled with guilt for so many reasons. Whenever there was an escape attempt, we would have to stand in our lines for hours and hours until the prisoner was brought back. If they didn't come back, prisoners were tortured and killed. She was afraid I was one of those people, that she was responsible for my death and possibly the death of others."

"I think I need a glass of water," I say. All this information is overwhelming.

"I'll be right back," says Tim. "Malka would you like some water?"

"Yes, thank you," she says with a weary smile. "Your husband, he is a kind man, I can tell."

"He really is. He reminds me of my father, actually," I say with a smile. "Malka, I'm sorry about how I reacted earlier – "

"Don't give it another thought. You were shocked. It's called bing *human*, dear," says Malka with a warm smile.

"You're very kind," I say. "A reunion after all these years..." I look at her and notice she has some of the same facial expressions as Mother.

"It's a miracle," says Malka. "A true miracle."

I smile at her, I can't help myself. I am happy for my mother, of course, but I can't help but wonder what life will be like now. I'm not a huge fan of change. Tim would say that's a *huge* understatement.

As if reading my mind, she says, "Everything is going to be fine, dear. Auntie Malka is here now."

I let out a laugh as Tim walks into the room. "Well," he says. "That's more like it."

"You said you had four children," said Tim. "Tell us about the others."

"Oh, well, Isaac is a neurosurgeon. He's married to Lydia. She is a real estate agent. They have three children, Jackson, Jillian and Jeffrey. Then there's Luke, he's a lawyer and he's married to Alexis, who is the office manager at his firm. They have twin daughters, Brigit and Chloe. My daughter Brooke is an elementary teacher and she's married to Griffin. They have three children, Brian, Mark and Amy. My daughter Katherine is a nurse and she is married to David, an orthopedic surgeon. They have two girls, Kendra and Lindsey."

"That's a big family," says Tim. "Never a dull moment, I imagine."

"No, never," she chuckles. "They are good kids, I am so proud of all of them. There is nothing like being a mother. And being a grandmother, well, what an extra blessing that is."

"I'm glad we got this chance to talk, it's nice getting to know you a bit," I say, and I mean it.

"You too. I'm so happy to have a niece. I look forward to meeting your children as well."

We return to Mother's room and find Dr. Krane has already left. Mother is beaming, as though she has some good news to share.

"Dr. Krane says I'm doing well," says Mother. "I may get to go home at the end of the week, isn't that wonderful?"

"I'm so happy for you, Sister," says Malka. She takes Mother's hand and gives it a squeeze. I can see how close they are, even after all these years it's as though they weren't apart one day. Maybe it's a sisterly thing, or maybe even a twin thing, but they have a bond that makes me wish I had a sibling myself.

"Isn't it too soon?" I ask. "I don't want you to push it, Mother, that's all. I want you to be ready."

"Of course, Olivia. Dr. Krane wouldn't let me go home unless he thought I was ready."

"She won't be alone, Olivia. I'll be staying with her so she won't overdo," says Malka. They begin to make their plans, talking excitedly. I look at Tim, and I know he's reading my mind. He walks over and puts his arm around me. I don't say anything, I just watch them. I have never seen my mother this way, so silly and carefree. This is all happening too fast.

15

Olivia

Dr. Krane enters the waiting room where Malka, Tim and I are waiting. He has just examined Mother. I know she is hoping he will let her go home soon. He walks up to Malka and shakes her hand. He congratulates us all on our newly expanded family.

Malka asks him how the examination went. He confirms that everything is looking great and is pleased with Mother's progress. Then something unexpected happens. Malka not only asks when Mother will be released but also if he feels Mother is up to meeting the rest of the family. This is all happening too fast. I have so many questions, only a few have been answered. Malka has told me a little bit about her past but I want to hear it from Mother, not *her*.

I can't help myself, I interrupt and wonder if it's too soon for both going home and the extended family visit. Again, Dr. Krane says he is pleased with her progress, and feels she is ready for both. Of course, I am glad she is recovering well, but to be honest I'm not ready for the other part – the extended family part. I need more time to adjust to Malka, not twenty or so more people.

Before I say something I might regret, I leave them to their discussion and walk into Mother's room. She looks so happy I don't want to ruin her mood. I pour her some ice water and sit on the edge of her bed. There is so much I want to say, so many questions I want to ask, but looking at my mother, all I can do is smile back at her.

16

Isaac

"You're home early, how was the hospital today?" asks Lydia as I walk into the foyer. A wonderful aroma is coming from the kitchen. My wife is an amazing cook and always greets me with a loving smile no matter what time I come home.

"Everything is fine at the hospital. I had surgery first thing this morning that lasted longer than I expected, almost seven hours, but very I'm very pleased with the outcome."

"That's wonderful honey, I had a great day myself – I sold the Bridgewater Estate today," says Lydia. I know she's pleased with herself; this estate will bring her a six-figure commission.

"That's *great*! We have a lot to celebrate tonight. I've called a family meeting and everyone will be here at seven. I have an announcement – a HUGE announcement. You're not going to believe this, but you're going to have to wait and hear with everyone else," I tease.

Not taking the bait, Lydia only smiles and returns to the kitchen. I run upstairs to take a quick shower, change into more casual clothes, and check my email.

Time got away from me, checking messages turned into over an hour of returning phone calls and replying to emails. When I return downstairs, the family is in the dining room. Somehow, Lydia has on the table enough food for an army, or at least our own small army. The aroma from the kitchen has vanished and our dining room table is covered with drinks, salad and several pizza boxes – the result of giving her about an hour to prepare for the entire family coming over. My wife is a saint, and I know how lucky I am.

"Hello everyone, I'm glad you could all make it. I'm going to get right to it. Mother called today, and she'll be spending more time in New York. She has asked me to cancel her return ticket. For now."

"What? Why would she do that?" asks Brooke, my most impatient sister.

"You're not going to believe this – she has found Nava." The room fills with gasps of surprise. We have heard about Nava our whole lives. The twin sister, the joy of our mother's life, the one question that needed to be answered – and now it has been.

"Isaac, how did this happen? Where did they find each other?" asks Lydia.

"Mother's speaking engagement, at the high school. As Mother walked onto the stage a member of the audience collapsed and was taken away by ambulance. You know how Mother is, she found out what hospital the woman was at, and went to visit."

"You're joking, right?" asks Luke. "This is unbelievable."

Just then my phone rang. "Perfect timing, it's her." I answer the phone. "Mother, we're all here and I just told everyone the wonderful news. You're on speaker."

"Hello family, isn't it wonderful? Isn't it just wonderful? I can't wait for you all to meet her." A chorus began, everyone talking at once.

"Whoah, hold on everyone," I say. "She can't decipher all the chatter! Mother, when are you coming home?"

"Actually, I have an idea. What would you all think of spending the holiday, here in New York? Hanukkah is in a couple weeks, the city is beautiful with all the lights, and you can meet Nava and her family. She has a daughter, Olivia, who's married with two children. Sadly, Nava's husband passed away several months ago."

"Hanukkah in the city, what do you guys think?" I ask. Again, the chorus.

"I know what I think," says Lydia. "I think the awesome commission I earned today will be treating us all to a lovely trip to New York!"

"Well, there you have it, Mother. We'll see you in a couple

weeks."

"I am so happy," says Mother. "I can't wait for you all to meet Nava. She's right here. Say hello Nava."

Silence fills the room and we hear a small voice on the speaker phone. "Hello, everyone. I can't wait to meet you all."

"We can't wait to meet you, Nava. We have heard all about you our whole lives. I can't imagine what you two must be feeling right now," I say.

"It was quite a shock of course," says Nava. "I keep pinching myself!"

"As do I, Sister," says Mother. "Isaac, I will talk to you all soon, we have to go now."

"Sounds good, Mother. Talk to you soon." I hang up the phone and look at my family. Everyone is cheering and embracing, so happy for this news. This wonderful news.

17

Abbie

I think my family has gone crazy. They're all acting weird, especially my parents. I keep coming home from school to an empty house with a note on the kitchen counter that says "We went to see Grandma, be back soon." *Gee, anyone ever think that I would like to go too?* I walk into my room and open my top dresser drawer. Inside there is an envelope where I keep some of my allowance. Eighty-four dollars. I have an idea.

After about twenty minutes, a cab is waiting in the driveway. Let my parents have a fit – I'm tired of wondering what's going on. Right now I am feeling brave but the closer I get to the hospital I begin to worry. I don't get into trouble, and I don't disobey my parents or make them worry about me. *There's a first time for everything, I guess.*

I step off of the elevator on Grandma's floor and walk down the hall. I pause outside of Grandma's room and look through the window. I see my parents, Grandma, and another woman is there too. She is sitting on Grandma's bed, holding her hand. They are laughing about something. Grandma looks so beautiful, so happy.

They don't hear me open the door. "Hi," I say. Everyone turns to look at me, shocked, as though I have interrupted something private.

"Honey," my Dad says. "What's going on? How did you get here?"

"Who's she?" I ask.

Grandma starts to answer but Dad cuts her off. "You are the one answering questions right now, so answer."

I look at the floor. "I wanted to see Grandma, so I took a cab."

"Is there someone downstairs waiting for cab fare?" he asks.

"No, I paid for it myself. Allowance," I say. I look over at my Mother, I can't tell if she's furious at me or proud of me.

"Sweetheart, come here," says Grandma. "I want you to meet someone."

I walk over to the end of the bed and look at this stranger. Maybe she's someone from Grandma's church. I know I've never met her but there's something familiar about her, like I should know her.

"Abbie, this is my sister, Malka." She is beaming, and so is Malka.

"It's so nice to meet you, Abbie, I've heard so much about you," says Malka.

"Um, nice to meet you too," is all I can manage to say. "I wish I could say the same, about hearing so much about you I mean. Grandma, I didn't know you had a sister."

"It's a long story, sweetie," says Grandma.

"Well I'd like to hear it, this long story," I say. "Where have you been? How come I didn't know you had a sister, Grandma?"

"Nava, let me," says Malka.

"Nava? Who's Nava?" I ask. I look at my parents, they are looking at me too but don't say anything.

"Nava is my birth name. Nava Shoshanna Prinz," says Grandma. "Malka is my twin sister."

"Twin? You don't look like twins," I say, though I see some resemblance in their eyes.

"Fraternal, not identical," says Grandma. "We were separated, during the war when we were just your age."

"*War*? Where were you, when you were separated?" I ask. I look at Grandma and then my parents and back again.

"Auschwitz," whispers Grandma, and she shares a look with Malka. The way they look at each other, their expressions, I see a resemblance.

Auschwitz? I immediately think of *Schindler's List*. I remember Grandma's reaction when she saw the DVD at her house that day we went to visit. It makes sense, her reaction. I see images of the movie in my mind. The soldiers, the camp, the striped uniforms, the trains, the torture. *Grandma and her sister survived that.* How? How did they survive that? They were my age, maybe even younger. I feel so foolish – things I have worried about, gotten upset about, things I wanted, things my parents and my grandparents have bought for me over the years because I *had* to have it. How selfish I have been!

I collapse on the end of the bed, sobbing and thinking of what Grandma went through as a girl. My father takes me in his arms and tries to soothe me, but I can't stop crying.

"That movie," I sob. "I remember your reaction when you saw it. I knew there was something wrong."

"Abbie, you didn't know," says Grandma.

"Why didn't I know? How come no one tells me anything? Mom, how come you didn't tell me, even when I told you about History Week, you didn't say anything?"

"She didn't know, sweetheart," says Grandma. "I have never spoken of my past to anyone, well, until now."

"Why not?" I ask her.

"When I came to America, I was determined to be a different person, to forget about my life during the war. America was to be a new beginning for me. I couldn't think of my past, it was too painful. Then there was the guilt, about not knowing for sure what had happened to Malka. I couldn't take it, I couldn't think about it, I couldn't speak of it."

"What about to Grandpa. Did you talk to him about it?"

"Not really, Abbie. He knew I was at the camp, but I never told him any details. He didn't want to know. He said that knowing the details would break his heart."

"That's a lot to keep inside, Grandma," I say. My anger has turned to sadness for her.

"It sure is," says Mom. My mother looks like she doesn't know how to feel – angry, sad, happy. She doesn't look like herself, she's not talking like herself. She looks exhausted, that is obvious.

"Does Alex know?" I ask, looking at my parents.

"We were going to tell you both, together," says Dad.

"Oh," I say. "I don't know what to say, Grandma. I want to say I'm sorry that you went through all that, but that sounds so lame now."

"It's not lame to feel compassion, sweetheart," says Grandma. "Come here, come sit with me."

I walk over to the bed and sit near her. She takes my hand. "I need you to forgive me," she says. "I need you *all* to forgive me, for keeping this secret from you. From all of you."

My mother shakes her head, folds her arms. "I need to absorb all of this, Mother. The past couple days, a lot has happened."

"Olivia, I know. But I am here, and I can see your mind, see all your questions just burning to come out, and I will answer them. Every single question you have, but not right now. I am so … tired."

"But Mother –"

"We understand," says Tim. "All this can be talked about later. Right now, your recovery is the most important thing. Right, everyone?"

"Yes, of course," says Mother. "We should go, so you can rest. Malka, would you like a ride to your hotel?"

"No, thank you. I'm going to stay here a bit longer," she says.

"She needs to rest, Malka," says Mother.

"I want her to stay, Olivia," says Grandma. "I need her to stay."

"Oh," says Mother. "Well, then by all means, stay." Mother walks out of the room. My father gives Grandma a kiss on the cheek and tells her they'll be back tomorrow. I walk over and give her a kiss as well. I smile at Malka and say goodbye. I run to catch up with my parents, who are walking towards the elevator. The ride down to the lobby is quiet, we're all in our own thoughts.

"Why does she want her to stay, and not me?" says Mother.

"It's not a competition, Liv," says my dad. "They have found each other again. Don't over-analyze. She's happy to have her sister back, that's all. It's nothing against you, you're her daughter and she's her sister, nothing more and nothing less."

"Why do I feel like I'm being shut out?" asks Mother.

"You really shouldn't. Let's all go home and have something to eat and then get some rest. Everything will be better in the morning."

18

Elizabeth

"Nava, this is lovely!" says Malka. It is almost seven in the evening, and I have finally been released from the hospital. After a few go-arounds, Olivia has agreed to let Malka and I stay at the penthouse alone.

"Thank you, I love living here. Would you like some tea? Or we could to go to bed, you look tired."

"Goodness, no. I couldn't possibly sleep right now. You look wonderful, sister. You must be so happy to be out of the hospital."

"Oh, yes. It's nice to be home. I'm so glad you're here."

"What do you think Olivia thinks about all this?" asks Malka.

"Malka, I don't even know what *I* think of all this. Honestly, I'm still in shock."

"She's very protective of you, your daughter?"

"Yes, I suppose she is. She is my whole world. This is all so unexpected, what has happened. I imagine she doesn't know what to think," I say and walk into the kitchen. I reach for the teapot to fill with water.

"Let me," says Malka. "I would think she would be excited for you, the whole family."

"Malka, I have to tell you something. Olivia had no idea of any of my past. *Nothing*."

"I know honey, you told me in the hospital, remember?"

"I remember, but when I say she didn't know anything, I mean *anything*."

"Nava, you survived the Holocaust – millions of people cannot say that. There should be no guilt or shame in that. I don't understand why you feel that way. Now that you're home we can talk about it, just the two of us. Help me understand, sister."

"I felt such guilt and shame, you're right. Not only because I survived, but because I thought I killed you."

"Listen to yourself. You did not kill me, and if I did not survive – which I *did* – it certainly wouldn't have been your fault. This is what you have thought all these years? That you killed me?"

"Yes! I escaped, I left you behind. I was so scared that you were punished and maybe even killed for what I did."

"Nava, not a lot of people knew we were sisters. We do not look alike, not really. We are not obvious twins, so to speak. Anyway, that is all behind us now. Here we are, reunited. We are together again, and we're both fine. We have so much to talk about."

"We do?"

"Of course we do! We have over sixty years to catch up on. Nava are you not thinking clearly? Are you all right?"

"Yes, yes, I'm fine. I'm just tired, and like I said, still in shock. Come with me, Malka, I'll show you the guest room."

"Thank you. Are you sure that's all? Are you feeling okay? You just got out of the hospital, and it's my job to make sure you don't overdo. Olivia will have my head if you overdo."

"I promise I am okay. I wouldn't dare to overdo, and Olivia will not have your head. Goodnight, sister. I am so glad you're here." We embrace, and I still cannot believe it's real. I enter my room and sit on the edge of the bed. I am exhausted, but the excitement is preventing my sleep. I lie on my side, thinking of a future that now includes my sister. My thoughts go to Olivia and then William. I wonder what he would think of all of this. I know in my heart he would be thrilled for me, and welcome my sister into our family and home with open arms. The last thing I see before I close my eyes is the loving face of my husband in a photograph on the nightstand. "Goodnight, my love," I whisper.

19

Elizabeth

The doctors and nurses took wonderful care of me in the hospital, but being out of that hospital has uplifted me. I know I have a lot of work ahead of me, and with Malka's help I know my recovery will be successful.

Malka and I share a lovely breakfast together. We don't talk much, we simply enjoy each other's company. Growing up, we didn't have to talk much, we had our own unspoken language. I could look at her and know what she was thinking.

I walk into the living room, and Malka is sitting on the sofa. My favorite book is on the end table, right where I left it. Malka makes some tea and brings it to me. "Mind if I sit with you and read?"

"Of course not, as long as you're really going to read and not hover."

"Don't be silly, I read every day."

We sit in silence for a few hours, feeling the warmth of the fireplace, hearing the crackling of the wood, engrossed in our stories. Out of the corner of my eye I could see the flames in the fireplace dancing. I look up and there is a glow in the room. It reminds me of evenings with William. He read his newspaper, and I a good book. We would each have a glass of wine on our respective end tables, and classical music played softly in the background. Once Olivia arrived our quiet evenings by the fire were often interrupted, and instead of reading the latest novel, I would hold her on my lap and sing her back to sleep so I could put her back in her bed. Wonderful memories.

"Penny for your thoughts, sister."

"I was just thinking about William. This is how we would spend many evenings, reading by the fire."

"Howard and I enjoyed doing that too, although with four children, it became more difficult. Finally, when all the children could read, we all would read together. I miss those days."

"Sounds lovely, I miss those days too," I say. Visions of those days are so vivid, so clear. They make me smile every time I think of them.

"Would you like to try a walk this afternoon? The sun is shining, and fresh air would do us both good. We wouldn't have to go far, as soon as you've had enough, we will come right back," she says.

"Yes, of course, sister, I love to walk."

"Well, great. Let's get ready then," she says and goes into the closet to get our coats. "The sun is out, but we still need to bundle up. Here you go," she says as she slides the coat up my arms. I pick out my favorite hat and scarf and smile at my sister. "Let's go," I say, happy to have this little outing with her.

The sun is deceiving, it's really cold outside, but I don't feel a thing, other than pure joy, that is. We walk along, arm in arm, looking into store windows. Malka sees a few things she likes, but we don't stop walking. We chatter constantly, just like we used to as girls.

After about an hour, I can feel myself needing to rest. I don't say anything, because I am enjoying myself so much, but my sister knows me very well."

"Time to go back," she says. "That's enough fun for today."

"All right sister, let's go back, but on the way we need to make one stop."

"Oh, really? Where?"

"You'll see," I tease. After about ten minutes, I see our destination. "There. We're stopping there."

"There? Well, all right!" says Malka. We stop at a hot dog stand on the corner of an intersection.

"Henry, hello," I say. "I'll take my usual, please."

"You got it, ma'am," says Henry with a smile. "And you? What can I get you today?" he asks Malka.

"I'll have what she's having, please," says Malka.

61

"Thanks, Henry," I say as I get him the money. "Keep the change, and I'll see you soon."

"Yes, ma'am. Thank you," he says and gives us a wave.

"Regular stop, sister?" says Malka.

"Oh, yes. For years now. William loved his hot dogs."

"Mmmm. I can see why," says Malka. "This is incredible – incredibly bad for us."

"Don't be silly," I say. "One hot dog every so often won't hurt anything." We share a laugh, because we know that this is one of those things that Olivia would be angry about.

"We're going to be in so much trouble, you know," says Malka.

"Well, *I'm* not going to tell her, are you? I ask.

"Hell no," says Malka. "No way!" We laugh so hard, our eyes water. What a wonderful way to spend an afternoon.

20

Elizabeth

"Malka, tell me about your speaking engagements. Was the panel at Abbie's school the first time you've done that?"

"Heavens no, I do several panels a year, all over the world," says Malka. "I have had wonderful experiences."

"Really?" I ask. "And people go to those kinds of things?"

"Yes, of course. It's a wonderful opportunity to educate people. Nava, there aren't a lot of survivors left. It's so important to keep our story going."

"Where do you go for these panels?" I ask.

"Schools mostly – high schools, universities, and some libraries. I do a lot of work at the Holocaust museum in Houston, and I have also been on television."

"Television? How did I miss that?" I ask. She must think I've been living under a rock for sixty years. I don't seem to know the kinds of things she does.

"Not primetime television, Nava. A local station did a special for the fiftieth anniversary. There were about twenty people on that panel. It was quite an experience. People ask a lot of great questions, they are fascinated with that part of history."

"I don't know if I could do that. Talk to people about my experience, that is. I certainly admire you for doing it though."

"Nava, tell me everything. I missed out on so much of your life. Tell me about your husband, about Olivia."

I open a cabinet and take out some photo albums. "Here, start with this one," I say, and hand her my wedding album.

"Look at you, Nava. What a beautiful bride you were! And William, so handsome."

"Yes, he really was. But more importantly, he was a beautiful man on the inside."

63

"You must have told him, right? About your past?"

"No, I didn't," I confess.

"Nava, you shock me – how could you not even tell your husband?"

I tell her about my wedding night. My sister has always been different than me. Open, even outspoken. No topic was ever off limits. I chuckle, because I realize that Olivia not only physically resembles her aunt, her personality resembles her as well.

"What's so funny?" she asks.

"I was just thinking, Olivia looks like you – and acts like you too."

"Well, we should get along just fine then," she says.

"Yes, perhaps you will when she calms down." As if on cue, the phone rings. I answer it in the living room.

"I'm coming over," says Olivia.

"No darling, that's not necessary right now. Let's have a family dinner tomorrow here at the penthouse."

"Family dinner, yes. I'm still coming over now, though."

"See you tomorrow, Olivia."

"Mother –"

"Tomorrow, Olivia. Today I am spending the day with my sister."

"Mother –"

"I love you so much, Olivia. Please give me this time with Malka. It has been over sixty years." I hang up. I have never hung up on her, and I immediately feel awful for doing so.

"Let me guess, that was Olivia," says Malka.

"How'd you guess?" We share a laugh. "My daughter, she doesn't know what to do with herself. I know her, she is feeling left out, and that is not my intention, but I just want to spend this time with you."

"And I with you, sister. I will stay as long as you need me to."

"I'm so happy to hear you say that," I confess.

"I have a surprise for you, sister. My daughter, Katherine has offered to take a leave of absence and come here to stay with us and help you with your recovery, would you like that?"

"Oh, no. She doesn't have to do that. That's too much to ask of someone, to drop everything and come here."

"She *offered*, Nava. She wants to come. She can be here tomorrow, just say the word. The rest of the family will be here in a couple weeks anyway."

"I don't know. Let me think about it. Right now we have to focus on tomorrow's dinner. We will need to go to the store today."

"Are you up to it?" asks Malka.

"I feel great, I promise. Just a quick trip and come right back."

"Which line do you take to get to the store?" she asks.

"Line? What do you mean?" I genuinely don't know what she's talking about, and it shows.

"Line – the subway. Which one do you take?"

"I've never been on a subway, Malka."

"You live in the city, Nava, of course you have. How do you get everywhere you need to go? You are full of surprises, aren't you?"

"Walk, of course. If it's raining, I take a taxi."

"You walk. How far away is the grocery store from here?"

"Not far, I love to walk. William and I walked everywhere."

"No subways, not ever?" I can see she is skeptical.

"Not ever. I was supposed to take the subway to Olivia's for Thanksgiving, but I couldn't do it, I couldn't walk down those stairs. A girl, a stranger, actually helped me back to my building."

"You poor thing. Are you ready to go?"

"Yes, let's go." We get on the elevator, and as we walk across the lobby, I am greeted by George, the doorman. "Mrs. McNamara, good morning."

"George, this is my sister, Malka. Malka this is George."

"Nice to meet you, George." My sister and I walk out into the sun, feeling the cold air.

"What a lovely day, a great day for *walking*, wouldn't you agree?"

"You are stubborn, Nava. Let's make a deal."

"A deal?"

"A compromise then. We will walk to the store, but we will take the subway back."

"Malka, no. Please don't make me do that."

"I will be right there with you. There are seats, and the trains are made of metal, or steel, or whatever they're made of, but they are not wooden, they are not cattle cars, Nava. Please let me help you face your fears. I am fortunate. I don't have them so I want to help you with yours. Please trust me."

"I – I will trust you."

21

Tim

"Hello, hello! Come in everyone," says Elizabeth, or Nava, I'm not sure what to call her now, to be honest. "Tim, good to see you. Abbie, give me a hug, sweetheart. You get taller every time I see you! Alex, you are tall enough, my dear."

"Hi Grandma," says Abbie. "We brought a cake."

"Wonderful! Please put it in the kitchen. Alex, where is your mother?"

"Well," says Alex, "She's –"

"Can I talk to you a moment?" I ask her. "In private."

"Sure, come into the study," she says, and I follow her down the hall.

"She's downstairs in the lobby. She's really upset. "She just wants to be included, you two have always been so close. Try to see it from her point of view."

"Tim, I understand. We're all getting used to each other. It's going to take longer than just a couple days for everything to fall into place."

"I know, I just wanted to let you know. You have all of our support, it's just hit Olivia really hard," I explain.

"Okay. Thanks, Tim. I'll go talk to her right now."

We walk into the kitchen, and to our surprise, Olivia is there, putting some shopping bags on the counter. "Hello, darling. I was just talking to Tim. How are you?"

"Great, Mother. Just great." Her sarcasm is noted, by everyone, and the chatter quickly stops.

"Is there something you want to say, Olivia? We're all family here, so if there is something you want to say, please say it." I look straight into her eyes, challenging her. This has never backfired in the past, and I am praying it doesn't now.

"No, Mother, nothing to say. What can I do to help?"

I let out my held breath. "We've got it under control, why don't we go into the living room for a little bit."

Of course, Malka knows nothing about our regular seating arrangement: Olivia and I on the loveseat, Tim in the recliner next to the fireplace, and the children on the large sofa. So when Malka sits down next to me on the loveseat, again I hold my breath. "Abbie, make room please," says Olivia, who sits on the large sofa with her children.

"I'm just dying to say something," says Malka. "I am so happy to be here with you all! I am so excited to get to know each of you, and tell you about my family back home. I'm just, well, I'm just so happy!" Malka takes Nava's hands in hers. "Nava, aren't you excited?" They both laugh, because this must be how they were when they were children. Everything was exciting, lighthearted and funny.

"You know, I just can't get over it," says Olivia. "Nava ... not Elizabeth. What happens now, are you going to change your name back to Nava? What do you want people to call you?"

"Liv ..." I say. "Please don't do this."

"No, it's okay, Tim," says Nava. "I will not change my name back to Nava, legally, after all these years of being Elizabeth, but I don't expect Malka to call me Elizabeth. She knows me as Nava, so that's what she will call me. Frankly, it's no one's business what my real name is, so my friends and your father's work associates will continue to know me as Elizabeth. I've thought about it and that's what I want to do."

"Okay, Mother," says Olivia. "I was just curious of what you were going to do now."

"That's fine. That's what I'm going to do."

"That's wonderful, sister," says Malka. "I don't know if I could call you Elizabeth, but I would have if that's what you wanted."

"That's sweet of you, but I would never ask you to use anything but my birth name. Now, tell us about your life back in Houston. How you came to the states and also about your lovely family. Tell us everything, sister."

"Well, after the war I ended up in an Army hospital. Oh, I was so sick. High fever, typhus, weak, hungry, thirsty. It took a long time for me to physically recover from the camp. I was there a few months."

"That's such a long time," says Abbie. "I don't like to go to a doctor appointment for an *hour*."

"Well, it wasn't all bad, Abbie. I met Dr. Joshua Howard there. Eventually, we were married and he brought me here to America, where he was from, originally."

"And where was that, exactly?" asks Olivia.

"Well, he was born in California, but we decided to go to Houston, since Joshua got a wonderful job offer at the Texas Children's Hospital in Houston. He was there for a long time, so passionate about his job. He was completely devoted to it, I was so proud of him and all his work."

"And you had how many children?" I ask.

"Four children – Isaac, Luke, Brooke and Katherine."

"I think it's wonderful that you have a son named Isaac, sister."

"Yes, I insisted our first boy be named Isaac."

"If Olivia were a boy that would have been her name also."

"Really?"

"Yes, of course. I wanted to honor our little brother."

"That's exactly how I felt. Joshua loved the idea. Isaac followed in his footsteps, he is a doctor as well."

"You must be so proud. What do your other children do?"

"Luke is a lawyer, Brooke is a teacher, and Katherine is a nurse. They have all done well, and they are all married with children of their own."

"Your husband must be proud too," said Abbie.

A look of sadness appeared on Malka's face. "Oh, I'm sorry," said Abbie.

"He passed almost ten years ago. The healer of many could not heal himself. Pancreatic cancer. It was a great loss to all of us. He was my first love, the father of my children. The heart of our family."

"Like my William," says Nava. She is almost in a trance. "I think I'll check on things in the kitchen."

We all sit down to dinner and I find myself looking at everyone at the table. Nava is at the other end of the table talking with Malka. Abbie is on my left and Alex is on my right. Olivia is to the left of her mother, looking so unsure of herself and her place in her mother's life. How can she not know that her mother's heart has room for both her and her sister? She has never had to share her, and now she doesn't know what to do. Just a few weeks ago my wife was stoic, confident. Now she is insecure and angry. I wish she would open her mind and her heart, but I know she has to do that in her own time.

"You will all be happy to know that Nava rode on a subway today," announced Malka. Everyone turned and looked at her in disbelief.

"Is that true, Mother?" asks Olivia.

"Well, yes. It's true."

"I can't believe it. You've never done that. You've always refused."

"I know, it was terrifying!"

"Your mother was very brave, Olivia," says Malka.

"Yes, I'm learning more and more just how brave and strong she is. Excuse me, I'm going to get dessert ready."

"Olivia, we haven't even finished our meal yet. Please, sit down. Why are you so angry?"

"I'm not angry, Mother. I have asked you a few times, not so long ago even, to take the subway to my home, and you wouldn't hear of it. Now, after what, *one day* with *her* you are riding the subway? How do you think I should feel about that, Mother?"

"Honey, please –" I say. "Now is not the time."

"No – *honey* – now is the perfect time. Why am I angry? I find out my mother, my best friend, has been living a completely double life for as long as I've known her. I thought I knew you, Mother, that we had no secrets. Now I know there are plenty of secrets. Then I get to a point where I feel like I finally know you, and then I find out there is yet another secret, only this secret is a human being. A sister – a *twin* sister – who is now here, which is wonderful, really, and suddenly I just don't know what to do with all these changes, and feelings, and I feel like I am losing the mother I just found. So I am truly sorry – so sorry, Mother – that I am angry, that I am not behaving the way I'm supposed to, I just don't know ..."

"Feel better, darling?"

"Well, yes. Yes I do, Mother. Thank you."

"Wonderful. Abbie, please pass the green beans."

22

Nava

"Well, that was quite an evening," says Malka. We are in the kitchen, doing dishes and putting things away.

"Yes, it was lovely, wasn't it?" I say, putting some plates in the cupboard.

"Lovely – really? Your daughter had a meltdown at the table, Nava." Malka puts some glasses in the dishwasher and starts wiping down the counter.

"Yes, she did. She said what she needed to say, she felt better, and the rest of the evening was lovely." I put the last of the pots and pans in their cupboard underneath the island and wipe down the top of the island. I put the floral bouquet she gave me in the hospital in the center of it, a doily in between them.

"Well, you certainly know how to handle your daughter," says Malka with a smile. She finishes wiping down the counter for me, always making sure I don't overdo.

"Many years of experience, sister. Olivia has a huge heart, and she speaks from there, not her head. I let her say what she needs to, she feels better – and sometimes foolish – and then things get back to normal. She just wants to be heard, so I hear her. She gets that from William. It's quite endearing once you get used to it. I think everything is cleaned up in here, how about some tea and television before bed?"

"Sure, the news should be coming on," says Malka. We sit down on the loveseat with our cups of tea as the headlines of the day are given.

"Come to Houston," says Malka. "Since Lydia has let me know the kids can't rearrange their testing schedules at school preventing them from coming for Hanukkah, I have thought of nothing else. Please, Nava, come to Houston. Meet my family."

I am excited and nervous all at once. It has been so long since I've been on a plane. I cannot help but think … what would Olivia say? I see Malka trying to read my mind.

"Well not now," she says. "When you are up to it, and when Dr. Krane says you're ready to travel. What do you think, will you come?" She looks so excited, and I am too, but meeting her family, her very large family – is it too much? I'm torn, I want to go, but I worry about my daughter's reaction. All these years, my world has centered around her, and William. This is something for just *me*. Oh, I really want to say yes.

"Well, I don't know. We will need to make arrangements," I finally say. "I need to –"

"Buy a plane ticket, Nava, that's all you need to do. Say yes and buy a ticket," she says excitedly.

"It's not that simple. There's Olivia –" I say. I regret the words as soon as I hear myself say them. This is not going to go over well with my sister.

"Back to Olivia, of course. Maybe you should call her right now and ask her permission to go somewhere," says Malka, and walks over to the window, looking down onto the street. I know she is frustrated.

"Whoah, Malka," I put down my tea. "That is uncalled for. I'll think about Houston, I will, but for now, I'm going to bed."

"Wait. Nava, please wait. I'm sorry. Let's talk about this," she says. She looks genuinely sorry.

"I will not be part of a tug-of-war, Malka. I do not have to ask her permission, but I will discuss it with her. That's just what we do, what we have always done. We discuss things, we make arrangements, because we care about each other, we respect each other."

"Okay, I guess I have a more 'relaxed' relationship with my family. I must admit you and your family are quite formal with each other. So proper, isn't it exhausting?"

"Exhausting? No, Malka, it's the way we are. Are you saying there is something wrong with –"

"I'm not saying anything, Nava, just that you and your family are different than me and my family. There is nothing wrong with either, it's just, different."

I stand and start to walk down the hall. I don't want to fight with my sister. "Goodnight, Malka. We'll talk more in the morning."

"Nava, I didn't mean anything by it."

"I know you didn't Malka. Really, it's fine. I'm tired and it's quite late. Sweet dreams, sister."

23

Olivia

When the phone rings this morning, I am hoping it is Mother; however, I quickly learn it isn't.

"Olivia, what is this I hear about your mother having a heart attack – weeks ago, I might add – and no one tells me about it?"

I close my eyes and take a deep breath. This is the last thing I want to deal with right now – or ever, for that matter. "Hello, Aunt Phyllis. Yes, Mother had a heart attack, but she's going to be fine."

"And no one called me because ..." she continues. As usual, it's all about *her*, and how it makes *her* feel. This woman is unbelievable.

"If no one called you, how do you know about it?" I ask, holding back no sarcasm.

"Tim called me this morning and told me. He couldn't talk long since he was at the office, but thought I should know. Did you not think I should know, Olivia?"

"Well, Phyllis, I've been a little busy, these past few weeks, so it wasn't at the top of my list, to be honest."

"Well, that's a fine attitude, isn't it," she snaps. "I don't think it's too much to ask to be kept informed about things."

"I have to ask, Phyllis, since when do you care about my mother? Thanksgiving Day you couldn't care less if she was there or not, you were much more concerned with the temperature of the turkey and how full your glass was with wine."

"Olivia, I have never heard you be so rude, what's gotten into you?" asks Aunt Phyllis.

"This is long overdue," I say, really not concerned with the consequence of my truth. "Since the day I have known you, you have been a pushy, rude, overwhelming busybody of a person, not to mention an obnoxious drunk. So that's what's gotten into me – goodbye, Aunt Phyllis, I have much more important things to do." I hang up the phone. "Take that you miserable bitch."

I put in a load of laundry and start to Swiffer the kitchen floor when the phone rings.

"Hello?" I say.

"Really, Olivia. Obnoxious drunk? Overwhelming busybody?" It's Tim, and he's not happy.

"Hi honey, how are you?" I ask.

"I've now been interrupted at work, *twice*. You know I'm on deadline, right?"

"Oh, I'm sorry," I say. "Did I interrupt you?"

"Don't give me that – you know exactly what I'm talking about," he says.

"I suppose I do, but what can I say? I just couldn't help myself. I am not going to be called by anyone – especially her – and belittled and reprimanded because I didn't call her right away to tell her about something she couldn't care less about. She doesn't care about Mother, never has. She wants gossip for her bridge club, and you should know that. She's *your* aunt."

"Technically, she's my aunt, but you know she's the one that raised me after my parents passed. I don't know what I would have done without her, Liv. Regardless of that, she's right, Liv. We should have called her."

"She's not right, and I can't believe you're taking her side on this, Tim. Give me a break, you know how she is. I'm surprised she was sober enough to remember what I said, and remember your number to call you back."

"Olivia –"

"I'm not kidding, Tim. She was slurring her words, and it's barely after breakfast time. I don't need her crap. I have enough to deal with without her trying to make me feel guilty."

"I get where you're coming from, and I'm always on *your* side, honey, you know that. Try to have a good day, okay? I'll see you tonight."

"Okay, I'll see you tonight. Oh, and honey?"
"Yes," says Tim.
"She had it coming."

24

Abbie

The six of us are sitting at the Olive Garden waiting for our dinner to arrive. Alex is rambling on about his exams and dad is working on his second bread stick. Mom has decided to have some wine with dinner, which is unlike her and Grandma is chatting with Malka.

"Olivia, I have something to discuss with you," says Grandma. "It may not be the best time, but we're all here together so maybe it is a good time."

"What is it, Mother. Is everything okay?" asks Mom.

"Everything is great, sweetheart. I just wanted to tell you that Malka has invited me to go to Houston."

"Out of the question, Mother. What are you thinking? You're not ready to travel," says Mom.

"Not *now*, Olivia. Once Dr. Krane gives me the go-ahead I would go. I want to meet the rest of my family. That's what I'm thinking."

"She would be well taken care of Olivia," says Malka. "She would stay with me at Isaac's home. She would have round-the-clock care if she needs it, and she wouldn't have to lift a finger. Lydia wouldn't hear of it."

"Round-the-clock care? If she is fit to travel, why would she need that?" asks Mom.

"My daughter, Katherine, is a nurse, and she would stay at Isaac's while Nava is there, just in case she needs anything. It would be a precaution, Olivia. I would have thought that would make you feel better."

"I don't feel good about her traveling, period," says Mom.

"If Dr. Krane gives her the go-ahead, it's really her decision, honey," says Tim. That got him a look, that's for sure.

At that moment, our waitress started handing out our meals. I love our waitress, she has great timing. She helps everyone with their grated cheese and before leaving us, asks if we need anything. I'm about to ask her to help my mother lighten up when dad says, "I think we're all set, thank you."

After a few minutes of eating Grandma announces, "I'm going to Houston. It's Dr. Krane's decision and it's my decision. I'm sorry if you don't like it, Olivia, but there is no reason for me not to go. I very much want to go, so I'm going."

Much to my surprise, Mom doesn't say anything. She just keeps eating, so the rest of us follow her lead. My father keeps looking at her, waiting for the bomb to drop, but she acts as though she didn't hear anything, though we all know she did. I guess the bomb will drop later.

25

Nava

"It's been such a long time since I've been on a plane," I say.

"You okay, Mother?" asks Olivia, sitting beside me.

"Just excited I guess. I'm glad you came with me. It's going to be a great trip."

"Are they meeting us at the airport?" asks Olivia.

"That's the plan, yes. I hope there are no delays, I don't want to keep them waiting too long."

"Everything should be on schedule, Mother. We left on time and it's a direct flight." She takes a magazine out of her knapsack and starts flipping through the pages.

"We left so early, I hope I didn't forget anything," I say. I haven't had to pack a suitcase in over twenty years. Everything William and I wanted to see was right here in New York. Friends, family, work, shopping, the park, and shows.

"How could you possibly forget anything? You probably started making your lists before we booked the flight," says Olivia. My daughter knows me too well.

"Well of course I did. It's really not that funny, Olivia, you can stop laughing now."

"I can't help it, Mother. Your little quirks make me laugh."

Suddenly, the plane jerked. "What was that?" I ask.

"Just a little turbulence. See? Back to normal," says Olivia, taking my hand.

"It's been such a long time since I've been on a plane," I say again and close my eyes.

"Mother, wake up. We're about to land," I hear Olivia's voice but it sounds so far away. "Mother, are you dreaming?" I open my eyes to my daughter's beautiful smile.

"Yes, a little. I'm glad we're here," I say, relieved that this flight is almost over.

"We're just about here, not quite. Feel the plane descending? Just a few more minutes."

"Are we on time?" I ask. I'm thinking of the rest of the family waiting in the airport.

"Yes, right on time, you dozed off for quite a while, do you feel better?"

"I do. I feel fine, Olivia. No need to worry about anything. I'm excited to be here in Houston."

"Grandma, have you ever been to Houston?" asks Abbie.

"No, sweetheart, this is my first time, just like you."

"I hope I like it," she says. "How long are we staying?"

"Abbie," says Olivia. "You know we're staying for a week. You seem nervous, what's the matter, honey?"

"I don't know. What if they don't like me?"

"Don't be silly, of course they'll like you. We're all going to have a great time," says Olivia.

"Are you trying to convince her or yourself," asks Tim.

"Don't start, okay? I'm trying to make the best of it," says Olivia, and puts her magazine and a water bottle into her knapsack.

"I'm not sure why you insisted we all come, we weren't even invited," he continued.

"Are you kidding me? One week with them, they'll have her moved to Houston and we won't see her again. I've got to keep this all in check, make sure she's thinking clearly and remembering who her *real* family is."

I couldn't listen to any more of this talk. "You do realize I can hear you two, right? I do not appreciate what you are saying, Olivia. I am not some child that is being babysat by you. I am perfectly capable of making decisions for myself."

"What's that supposed to mean? She's already asked you, hasn't she? This is unbelievable!" I can see she's already getting worked up. That look comes over her, like a tiger in the tall grass, waiting and watching, ready to pounce on its prey.

"My dear, you need to calm down. She has not asked me to

move to Houston, and she is my real family too. She is my sister and your aunt. If your sole purpose for coming on this trip was to get to know my sister and her family then by all means you stay. If your purpose is to babysit then you can get on another plane and go back to New York. Do you understand me?"

"All right, you two," says Tim. "We haven't even gotten off the plane yet. What a way to start a vacation. Maybe we should get another plane and go home, if this is how it's going to be all week."

We sit in silence until the plane lands. *Please, God, let this week go well. Please keep my daughter's mind and heart open, and show her that our family is growing, not falling apart. And God? Please don't let my sister be too angry that I didn't come alone.*

26

Nava

"My, what a large airport. I hope we can find them all right. Look at all these people!" I feel a little overwhelmed, looking around.

"Well, it is Saturday, Mother, a popular travel day. Just take your time, we'll find them," says Olivia.

Walking through the airport, making our way through the crowd, suddenly everything turns to black and white and goes into slow motion. People off to the right, standing in line, somber faces. In a flash, they are all wearing striped uniforms, standing in line for cold coffee and moldy bread. I look to the left, and a group of people with their backs towards me are slowly walking away. I see a woman, she has the same build and coat as – "Mother, where are you going? Mother, come back!"

"Mother, are you all right? Who are you talking to?" asks Olivia with concern on her face.

"Look, don't you see? She's walking away! She's walking to the left – I don't understand, why can't you see what I see? Oh no ... she's gone. She's gone," and with that, I realize that my mind is playing tricks on me and I begin to sob. Tim takes me into his arms and we walk over to some empty seats.

"Here, Grandma, have some water," says Abbie. She hands me a bottle of water.

"Thank you, sweetheart. I need a restroom. My sister cannot see me like this."

"Over there, Mother. Come on, we'll get you freshened up," says Olivia. There is a long line. "Pardon us, we just need to get to a sink," she says, and women allow us to pass.

I am splashing water on my face, but the tears have left my

eyes red. "Malka cannot see me this way."

"Would you just forget her for *one second*? What happened out there, Mother? Are you sure this trip is a good idea? Let's go home." Olivia is coming my hair behind me, looking at me in the mirror.

"Absolutely not. First of all, I will not forget her, not for one second – she was gone from my life for a long time. Try to imagine what that must be like for me. Not for *you*, for *me*. I know you're having a hard time with all of this and I am truly sorry for that, but this is what life *is*, Olivia. It's gray, it's messy, it's the unexpected comings and goings of people and events. I blame myself. You were raised in a bubble. That's my fault, not yours. I am so sorry, Olivia."

"No, I'm the one that's sorry. I am having a hard time but I'm certainly not making it easier for anybody. Let's just try to have a good time, okay? Are you ready to get out of here? I think these people have heard enough, don't you?"

I look around and see we have put on quite a show for absolute strangers. I am embarrassed and very much want to get out of here. "Yes, I suppose they have. Excuse us, I apologize. Very sorry," I say, and we return to Tim and the kids.

"Everything okay?" asks Tim.

"Fine, let's get the bags," says Olivia.

"Already done. See?" He steps aside and there is the luggage. I was relieved to be able to avoid another line.

"Any signs of Malka yet?" I start to look around, but this time, people are walking quickly, in regular clothes going about their business. I smile, because it's nice to see things for how they really are. "Let's just keep walking, she is here somewhere."

After a few minutes, I notice a large, colorful sign "Welcome Nava!" A large group of people, Malka front and center, are looking our way, beaming. "There she is! Nava, you're here!"

I run to her, "Yes, sister," and we embrace. "What a beautiful sign – that's quite a welcome. Thank you so much, I love it."

"The children made it. We're all here – come meet the

family!" says Malka.

"Hello, Malka," I hear behind me. It's Olivia, reminding me that I didn't come alone.

"Olivia, what a surprise! Hello again, Tim, kids," says Malka. "I wish I had known you were coming. No problem, we'll figure out arrangements later. Come meet the family – they can't wait."

"My goodness," I say. "What a beautiful looking family." They really were, they were all stunning. Nicely dressed, well groomed. No wonder she was proud. One by one I am introduced.

"Nava, this is Isaac. His wife, Lydia, sons Jackson and Jeffrey, and daughter Jillian." I was overwhelmed with emotion, and as I embraced them all, I felt so welcomed into this family. What a joy.

"It is so nice to meet you, Isaac. You honor our brother. He would be so proud to have you as a nephew. You have a beautiful family," I say. My face almost hurts from smiling so much.

"Thank you, Aunt Nava. The pleasure is ours, really," says Isaac. "Welcome to Houston."

"Aunt Nava," I say. "I love the sound of that."

"This is Luke, his wife Alexis and daughters Brigit and Chloe."

"So nice to meet you. Twins, how wonderful!" Again, I am embraced.

"Nava, this is my daughter, Brooke. Her husband Griffin, and sons Brian and Mark, and daughter Amy." I don't think I have ever hugged so much in my life, and it feels so good.

"So nice to meet you. You're the teacher, am I right?" I ask.

"Yes, that's right. I teach elementary school here in the city," says Brooke. We embrace as well. Malka's children are very affectionate. They get that from their mother.

"That's wonderful, just wonderful," there is no job more important than teaching our children," I say. "Well, besides raising children, that is." Brooke agrees.

"Last, and not least, this is my daughter, Katherine, her husband David, and daughters Kendra and Lindsey."

"Yes, Katherine. I want to thank you for offering to come to New York to help me with my recovery. That was so sweet of you," I say.

"Oh, don't mention it," says Katherine. "I would have loved to be of help, but Mother says you did great with your outpatient physical therapy. You look wonderful, the picture of perfect health."

"You're too kind. This is all so wonderful to meet you all. Please, everyone, meet my daughter, Olivia, her husband Tim, and their children Alex and Abbie."

We form a large group, chatting away as if this wasn't our first meeting. I am so happy we are all here together. I have this strange feeling come over me, as though my life is just beginning in some way.

"I think it's time we get out of this airport," says Isaac. "The bus is right outside."

27

Tim

"What a great idea, to rent a bus," I say to Alex.

"It's not a rental," chuckles Jackson. "It's my father's. He bought it a few years ago so the whole family could travel together."

"He bought a bus?" asks Alex. "Just so you could travel together? How often do you use it?"

"A few times a year," says Jackson.

"That's it?" asks Alex. He looks surprised.

"Why do you look so surprised? How do you and your family travel?" asks Jackson.

"Well, either we drive or go by airplane, of course," says Alex. He and Abbie meet eyes. "There is only five of us, including our Grandmother. We don't need a big bus like this to travel."

"I suppose not," says Jeffrey. "There is eighteen of us, nineteen when our Grandmother comes with us, so we really need the room. Don't look so impressed, Alex. It's only a bus."

"Well, I am impressed. This isn't an ordinary bus, it looks more like something a celebrity would have." I enjoy watching my son interact with his cousins. Ordinarily, he is quite shy and soft-spoken. I am glad he feels comfortable to have a conversation without my prompting. He is holding his own with his cousins, who have obviously lived a privileged life so far. Our family is quite well-off, but Olivia and I have raised the kids to be very down-to-earth and not focus on materialistic things. Family is our priority, for sure.

"My father is kind of a celebrity, I guess," says Jackson. "He is a very popular doctor here in Houston, he's won a lot of awards. And of course Grandmother is known all over the place

87

for all that she does at the museum and all that."

"What does she do at a museum?" asks Abbie.

"It's more like what she doesn't do – she helps out, she sits on panels, she brings in funds to maintain it, she travels to educate people about the Holocaust. She's quite amazing," says Jillian. "She is an inspiration to many people, and she has more energy than we know what to do with. We're all very proud of her."

"I can tell," says Alex. "So you have known about her past all along?"

"Yes, of course," says Jackson. "We all know her story, and we know all about her family, especially Aunt Nava. I feel like I've known her all my life, and I just met her today."

"Really. You feel that way too?" asks Alex.

"Sure," says Jillian. "We all do. She has always told us about her life with her twin sister, what fun they had as children right up to their separation at the camp. Heartbreaking, really. She has always said that she didn't know for sure, but she thought she would feel it in her heart if Nava had died or not. She told us that she has always hoped that her sister was alive, somewhere, and maybe they would meet one day."

"She has dreamed of a reunion for such a long time," says Jackson. "I think that's why she was always so eager to go to forums and speak on panels and any other event having to do with the Holocaust. I think her reunion with Aunt Nava is the result of years and years of prayer."

"I don't know what to say," says Alex. "I guess you were raised very different than we were."

"Look," says Jackson. "We know your Grandmother kept her past to herself until recently. That doesn't make her a bad person – Grandmother has told us that many survivors couldn't or wouldn't talk about their past once they began a new life. She's just so happy that she's found her sister, alive and well. She says she wants to spend the rest of her days with her."

"In New York?" asks Abbie.

"No, here in Houston," says Jillian. "With us."

"I don't know about that," says Alex. "She wouldn't leave us and move out here, isn't that right, Abbie?"

"I hope not, I want her in New York. I can't even imagine what Mom would do or say if Grandma moved away. She would be devastated."

"She could move here too, if she wanted. All of you could," says Jillian.

"I can tell you right now, I'm not leaving NYU. Mom and Dad, they love New York. Grandma loves New York. She won't even move in with us because she won't leave the penthouse where she and Grandpa lived together. She isn't going anywhere."

Jackson and Jillian looked at each other and smiled. "Well, we'll see, right?" says Jillian. "It's up to her anyway; she's certainly old enough to decide where she lives. I make my own decisions and I'm twenty-four. I love it that way."

"Like I said," says Alex. "We were raised very differently."

"What are you guys talking about," I ask. I realize I have tuned out the kids' conversation and have been staring out the window for quite some time. I also realize we've been on this bus for a long time, almost two hours.

"Nothing important, Dad," says Alex.

The bus slows down as it makes its way up a winding driveway.

28

Nava

"Home at last," says Lydia. "So nice to be home."

"All right everyone, here we are," says Isaac. He stands up and goes to the seat behind him. "Mother, let me take your arm." He guides Malka out of the bus, so gentle with his mother.

As I step onto the cobblestone driveway, I can't help but gasp. In the center of the driveway is a large water fountain, and the house isn't a regular house, it's a mansion. Pillars, huge potted plants, manicured lawn, stone walls, and lovely tall trees. Coming from the back of the house was a wonderful smell, like a barbeque. I look into the sky, and see smoke rising above the tall roof. Everything turns to black and white, and falling from the sky is gray snow coming out of a brick chimney.

"Aunt Nava," says Isaac. "Do you need some help?"

I snap out of my daydream. "No, I was just looking at the house. Isaac, this is a beautiful property."

"Thanks Aunt Nava, we like it," he says with a look of pride.

"How long have you lived here?" I ask. I'm still looking around, in awe of the perfection of this place.

"Almost six years now. Lydia found it," says Isaac.

"Well, it's just beautiful. You should be very proud," I say, and take his arm.

"Thanks," says Isaac. "All right everyone, let's head inside."

Everyone makes their way through the large front doors and into the grand foyer. Again, I couldn't believe my eyes. This looks more like a hotel than a home, but at the same time it is very welcoming and intimate.

"Sister, isn't it beautiful?" asks Malka. "I just love it here. I think you will too. Wait until you see our suite."

"Suite?" I ask. This is all too much. As wonderful as my life has been since I married William, I am almost intimidated by my nephew's life.

"A Hanukkah present for the both of us. Come with me, you're going to love it," says Malka.

"For the both of us? But I just met him today," I say.

"That's Isaac – very loving, very generous. Very much like his father," says Malka. She is beaming.

As I make my way up the staircase, I look down into the foyer. I am happy to see Tim talking with Luke and Griffin, but behind him I see my daughter, looking intimidated and out of place. "Olivia," I call down. "Would –"

"We'll be right back," calls Malka. She takes my hand and leads me up the rest of the staircase.

"What did you do that for?" I ask, a little confused.

"Nava, I have to ask, and please don't take it the wrong way, but why didn't you come on your own?"

"Well, we just thought it would be best if they came along. Olivia says at my age, especially with the surgery, the hospital stay and cardiac rehab, that I shouldn't travel this far alone."

And what did *you* say, sister?"

"I'm sorry I didn't tell you she was coming. I hope I'm not putting anyone out."

"I don't think that's the problem, Mother." We turn around and at the top of the stairs is Olivia. The look on her face told me she heard everything Malka and I had said. "My children had a conversation on the bus with Jackson and Jillian, and apparently the big plan here is to have you move to Houston, permanently. Isn't that right, Malka?"

"It's no secret that I would love to spend more time with my sister, Olivia, it should be surprising to no one. Not even to you."

"Not even to *me*? What is that supposed to mean?"

"Oh good, you're up here already," says Isaac. "Aunt Nava, I want to show you your belated Hanukkah present. It's for you and Mom, really. I hope you like it." He opens the tall double doors in one swoop and the sun comes pouring out into the hallway.

"Oh my," I put my hand over my mouth in disbelief.

"I told you you'd love it," says Malka. "Come on in, you need to see everything he's done for us. It's amazing."

As I walk into the room I look to the left. On the wall there are four large black and white photos. I look at Malka. "I know," she says. "My son found these for me and had them enlarged."

The first photograph is my parents' wedding picture. My beautiful mother, how I miss her so. My father, in his suit, looking so happy and proud. "I love that picture, Isaac. Where did you get it?"

"Lydia and I made a project of finding some things for Mom. We made phone calls, wrote letters, did some research on the internet – it took months, even years, to track some of these things down. Some things she has already seen, and some we kept as a surprise, since we knew she would be coming to live with us eventually. Last fall she finally agreed to move in with us. She had a room down the hall, but while she was in New York with you, I had this renovation done."

"Nava, isn't this wonderful? Look – that's you and me." The second photo was a picture of the two of us. We were all dressed up in our ruffled dresses, I with my hair down held only with a headband; Malka with her two braids and ribbons. "I remember this day, don't you?"

"Oh yes. Uncle Simon and Helena's wedding. Such a wonderful celebration."

"We looked so pretty, didn't we?" asks Malka.

"Yes," I chuckled. "We looked just fine."

The third picture was of our building – Father's accounting firm on the ground floor, and our apartment on the second floor. "He worked so hard, didn't he? To start the firm and give us a beautiful apartment to live in. The good old days, I like to call them," says Malka.

"I loved that apartment, I miss it. I miss all the good times we had there, before the war started," I say. In my mind, I can see the old neighborhood, people walking down the street, with yellow stars on their clothing, soldiers walking on the sidewalk, watching everyone very closely. Eyes of stone, no emotion, other than perhaps hate. I snap out of my daydream.

"Yes, those were wonderful days – before the war, of course."

"Nava, they found Shoshanna," says Malka. She is holding my hand, and gives it a little squeeze, as though trying to help me remember.

"What? No –" This is incredible news. My dear friend, still alive!

"Yes, they did. She is in England now, living with her daughter, Helene. We write back and forth now, and I have spoken to her on the phone as well."

"She survived, how wonderful!" I hold my face with my hands, still amazed at this news.

"Who is Shoshanna?" asks Olivia.

"She was our good friend and neighbor. Her father worked in Father's firm. They were like family," says Malka.

"She was like having another sister, right Malka?" I ask, knowing the answer.

"Oh, yes. I loved the way she fixed my hair, how she would be the teacher when we played school and we were the students."

"So many afternoons, playing school," I said. "Wonderful memories."

"Nava, let's call her tomorrow. I know she would love to hear your voice after all these years."

"Could we? I would love that."

"With the time difference, we should call in the morning," says Malka. Isaac nods in agreement.

"Oh, I can't wait to speak to her. This is wonderful, I'm so happy!" I take a few steps. "Look at that, I can't believe they found that."

The fourth photograph was of our whole family. Malka and I are standing in front of our parents. It was taken about a year before we had to leave our home. The style of dress mother was wearing showed it was a maternity dress with our little brother

93

inside.

The next wall has two floor-to-ceiling windows with the most beautiful floral draperies with burgundy braided tie-backs. In between is a fireplace with a beautiful mantel with more photographs on it. Above, a floral swag with the same color theme as the curtains. The carpet is a plush cream color, the walls a warm cinnamon brown. In front of the windows are oversized chairs, perfect for reading, or to look at the giant flat-screen television hanging on the opposite wall.

The third wall, which would be to the right when you entered the room is an entryway to the bedrooms. One of them looks like it is already 'lived in' so we know that is Malka's room. To the right is another room, also beautifully decorated. A queen size bed with burgundy bedding. The floor and walls a pristine white with more photographs on the walls.

"This is your room, Nava. I hope you like it," says Isaac.

"It's so lovely, Isaac, you shouldn't have," I say, and give him a hug. "Thank you, so much."

"It's our pleasure. You will always have a home here in Houston, Aunt Nava."

"Her home is in New York," says Olivia. "Am I right, Mother?"

"I am a blessed woman, Olivia. I have two homes now." Malka puts her arm around me, smiling.

"I would love for you to spend as much time here as you can, sister. I just want to spend time with you. I hope that's all right," says Malka.

"Of course it is, I want the same thing. But like I said before, I will not be in the middle of a tug of war, that's not fair to anybody, and I just won't do it. This is not a competition, and I am not a prize to be won. I will spend time with *everyone* in my family as much as I can. Understood? Olivia? Malka?"

"Of course, sister. That's all I want, some of your time. We lost so many years together."

Olivia looks around the room and then at me. She shakes her head and walks out of the room.

"Olivia?" I turn back to Malka and Isaac. "I'm sorry. She's having a hard time with all of this. She'll come around. I hope she comes around, that would certainly make things a lot easier."

"Mr. Howard," a voice called from the doorway. "Lunch is ready."

"Thank you, Nina, we're on our way," says Isaac. "That's Nina, one of the staff." Nina says hello, then leaves the room to go downstairs.

"How many people are on your staff?" I ask. It is all overwhelming – the size of this house, the staff, the suite, everyone here. It's organized chaos, and I'm having the time of my life. I wish my daughter could be happy too, that she would let herself go, relax a little and get to know her extended family. Brooke and Katherine are close to her age, and she could have a wonderful friendship with them especially, if she would just let it happen.

"We have five wonderful people working here. We couldn't run this house without them," says Isaac.

In the back yard there is a large white tent, and from it comes a wonderful smell, which reminds me how hungry I am. The tent is closed in, but stepping inside it looks like a formal restaurant. Several tables with white linens, floral centerpieces, and glowing candles.

To the left is a long table containing a wonderful barbeque buffet, with staff there to assist us. In each corner there is a fireplace to keep us all warm. It's an amazing transformation.

"Dad loves his barbeques, Aunt Nava. We have them every week all winter long. The whole family comes, and it's a great time," says Jeffrey.

"Your father is quite remarkable," I say, following him further inside.

"Nava, sit over here with me, will you?" asks Malka.

"Of course, I was just looking for Olivia."

"She's over there with Brooke, she's fine," says Malka.

I look around the room until I see her, and sure enough she's talking with Brooke, and she's actually smiling. Maybe she'll come around after all. When our eyes met, she is smiling, but her eyes tell a different story. She looks lost, and I have never seen her this way, so outside of herself, so awkward.

"Hi, can I talk to you for a minute? Over here?" asks Tim.

"Of course. Isn't this something?" I ask him, taking his arm and walking to a space away from everyone else.

"It is, but I don't think we're going to stay. I don't like seeing Olivia this way – I think I should take her home."

"Tim, we just got here, and I think it would be good for you all to stay. Get to know our extended family," I say.

"I don't think she's ready. Look at her, she's not herself," says Tim.

I turn to look at him. "I know, but taking her home isn't going to help, Tim. She needs to work through this here, not alone. If you leave now, what would be resolved? Nothing. Please, stay. It's going to be all right. She needs to be here."

I leave Tim and walk over to Olivia. "Hello, sweetheart. Our table is over here, come sit with me."

"Aunt Nava, I'm so glad you're here," says Katherine. "I look forward to getting to know you better."

"Thank you, Katherine, that's so sweet of you to say. I look forward to getting to know you as well."

I take Olivia by the arm and walk to our table. Everyone is sitting at their table, getting ready to eat.

"Let's all raise our glasses, be it wine or chocolate milk, and toast the arrival of our Aunt Nava," says Isaac. "It is a miracle that you are here with us, reunited with your family."

"That's it," says Olivia, slamming her glass on the table. "Her family? Like she didn't have one before she came *here*? Enough is enough. Tim, you mentioned going home earlier, I want to do that. Now."

"Olivia, please. It's a toast. They're glad we're here," I say, trying to diffuse Olivia's anger.

"No, Mother. They're glad *you're* here. They couldn't care less if I'm here or not. We are barely acknowledged and when we are it's as if we're some annoying appendage of you."

"Olivia, that's just not true. Maybe it would help if you just lightened up a little bit, and enjoy yourself."

"Aunt Nava, would you come and say a few words?" asks Isaac. He seems oblivious to Olivia's anger, and I am thankful for that.

I make my way to Isaac's side and take the microphone he hands me. I take a deep breath, I am not a public speaker. "I am overwhelmed as I look at all of you. The recent weeks have changed my life forever. This is all the result of a chance meeting and I have my granddaughter to thank for that. Abbie convinced me to attend a panel at her school. This toast should be for her, not me. My daughter, her family and I are pleased to be here and we look forward to getting to know you all better. I want to thank you for welcoming us into your beautiful home, Isaac and Lydia. I don't know what else to say, it's just very overwhelming, in a good way. Thank you all, so much, for embracing us into your family."

"Mother? Your turn, I know you have something to say!" says Isaac.

Malka comes to my side and puts her arm around me. "I have spoken of my sister to you your whole lives. I am glad you are now able to know her in person, not just through my stories. It means the world to me that we have been reunited. I know you are overwhelmed, sister, but I am right here by your side. I love you so very, very much!" We embrace as sisters do, and I am elated with her words. I look into her eyes and I am taken right back to our days in the field, playing and singing. We are old women now, but she makes me feel like a young girl, young and free.

29

Nava

The next morning I wake to a knock on my bedroom door. It's Lydia, all dressed. "Good morning, Aunt Nava. Would you like to join us for breakfast?"

"What time is it, did I oversleep?" I ask, sitting up in my bed.

"Of course not," she says. "I'm an early riser, it's only seven. Breakfast is at eight."

"I will see you at eight then. Thank you, Lydia, for everything. This suite is just beautiful."

"I'm glad you like it. I'm going to help your sister now. See you downstairs."

"Help Malka? Is she all right?" I ask.

"Sure. She has some arthritis, so I just give her a little help in the morning. Nothing to worry about, I promise."

"Let me put on my robe, I'll give you a hand," I say. I don't remember her needing help in the morning when she stayed with me in New York. I hope she took care of herself while she took care of me.

As I enter Malka's room, I see her sitting on the edge of her bed. She looks like she is in a lot of pain. Her face looks strained as she looks up at Lydia, almost helpless. We are twins, yet somehow she seems much older than I. She turns her head and sees me. "Oh, Nava. I don't want you to see me like this."

"Here's your pills," says Lydia. She is holding a small tray with a glass of orange juice and some medication. "Soon you'll feel much better."

"Malka, don't be silly. See you like what? So you need some medication, there's nothing wrong with that. As long as it helps, right?"

"My body can't keep up with my mind. I get so frustrated. I

know I'm an old woman, Nava, but I'm not ready to act or feel like one."

"Nonsense," says Lydia. "You get your little boost in the morning and then you run circles around everyone the rest of the day. Don't believe a word she says, Nava," and with a big and beautiful smile, Lydia leaves the room carrying the little medicine tray. "See you two in a little bit."

"Thank you, Lydia," says Malka. "That girl is a dream, Nava. I couldn't ask for a better daughter-in-law. Isaac made such a wonderful choice marrying her. I never worry about my son or my grandchildren's happiness, knowing she is here with them. She does it all – takes care of Isaac, the kids, and on top of all that, she's a very successful real estate broker. She juggles so much, and as you see, she does it all with a smile on her face. She is just endless energy."

"Yes, she seems wonderful. Everyone here is, well, wonderful. I'm going to get dressed. Are you all right for a few minutes?"

"I'm fine, my 'little boost' as Lydia likes to call it, is starting to work. Don't worry, Nava. You're lucky you don't have these aches and pains – or do you?"

"My time will come, Malka, don't you worry."

"And when it does, Lydia will have two glasses of juice on her tray and even more pills."

"Gee, isn't that something to look forward to," I say as I leave the room. I lift my suitcase, and it's empty. Nina must have unpacked my things when I was at dinner last night. I open the closet and sure enough, my clothing is neatly on hangers and on the floor is the two pairs of shoes I brought. I open the dresser drawer, more clothes. I walk into the bathroom and my toiletries are all set up for me.

As Malka and I enter the dining room, everyone is already there. The chatter and laughter and clinks of silverware is music to my ears. I stand in the doorway and just take it all in. The sun is shining through the windows, there are fresh flowers in the center of the huge table and on both sides of the bouquet is enough to feed, well, us.

"Good morning, Mother," says Isaac, and he gives her a kiss on her cheek. "Good morning, Aunt Nava," he says and gives me a kiss as well. "Did you sleep all right? How is the mattress, were you comfortable?"

"Yes, everything is perfect, thank you so much. I haven't slept that well in a long time. Perhaps it's time for a new mattress in New York."

Isaac and Malka share a look but don't say anything.

"Sit down, ladies," says Lydia. "Get it while it's hot." I know she said earlier that Malka runs circles around everyone, but so far the only one I see running around is Lydia and Nina. I admire the way Lydia is hands-on with everything. She has a staff, but she works just as hard as they do. She doesn't sit there and let them do everything. I have never seen that before, but I like what I see here.

"This all looks so delicious. This is breakfast every morning?" I ask.

"No, not all the time. Usually the whole family isn't here, but Malka, Isaac, the kids and I do have breakfast every morning together. It's a good way to start the day," says Lydia.

Pancakes, fruit, and tea were enough for me, but there was also eggs, French toast, cereal, bagels, yogurt, and regular toast for everyone. By the time breakfast was over there was barely a crumb left. I couldn't believe my eyes!

"I'll see you all later, I have rounds at the hospital." A chorus of goodbyes and have a good day begin. "What time are we due at the museum?" Isaac asks Lydia.

"Seven-thirty, so dinner will be early tonight. Can you be home by five?" asks Lydia.

"Shouldn't be a problem. Rounds, then only two surgeries today. See you later, love," and he breezes out the door.

"All right," says Lydia. "I'll get this cleaned up and then we can plan our day. Nava, would you like to do some shopping?"

"Oh, I don't think there's anything I need, but thank you," I say.

"I thought maybe you'd like a new dress for tonight," she says.

I look at Malka. "I'm speaking at the museum tonight," she says.

"Really? That's exciting. I did bring a couple dresses just in case. I tend to over pack. Right Oliv – where did Olivia go?"

"She's outside with Tim and the kids. I guess they wanted some fresh air. We got a little snow last night, and with the sun, it's really pretty out there."

I walk over to the window, and I can't help but laugh. "Look, they're actually building a snowman. I haven't seen Olivia do that in years."

"Has she always been this way, Aunt Nava?" asks Katherine. "Unhappy?"

"No, of course not. She has had a lot of changes to deal with recently, a lot to accept. Look at her out there, that's my Olivia. I'm to blame for all this and I need to fix it, so she can forgive me and be happy again."

"Nava, I'm not going to stand here and listen to you blame yourself for everything," says Malka. "Olivia has had plenty of time to listen to you, to forgive you, to accept things as they are now. She is responsible for her behavior, not you. I can't listen to you blame yourself over and over again. It's just not right, sister."

"What's not right is what I've done. I kept my secrets for so long, how could I do that to her? And what if I had never told her? What if I had never gone to that panel and saw your name in the program? I would have died not knowing what happened to you. Have you thought of that? I have."

"Nava, everything happened the way it was supposed to. You are here with me, right where you should be. Let's go shopping today, just us girls. We'll get some lunch and then have a wonderful night at the museum. Okay?"

"Yes, of course," I say. "Let's go shopping."

"What's going on?" I turn to see Olivia in the doorway.

"We're going shopping. I want you to go with us," I say.

A few minutes later we are on our way to Macy's on West Alabama Street. It's a beautiful day and everyone is excited for this little adventure. Houston is a big, beautiful and busy city, and so far I am really enjoying this trip. I have to admit I'm grateful Olivia is in a different car for this trip. It will be good for her to get to know Katherine, Brooke, Alexis and Brigit. Malka and I have a wonderful conversation about her speaking engagement tonight. I am so proud of her for all that she does. I wish I were more outgoing, more open to speak of what happened to me in public. Maybe tonight will be a learning experience for me as well.

"Oh, I love this store!" says Lydia.

"I bet Isaac doesn't when the bill comes in," jokes Katherine.

"Bite your tongue, Kat, I have plenty of money of my own. I can treat myself if I wish, don't you agree?"

"We have been blessed," says Malka. "No more talk of money. Let's just have some fun."

"So tell me, Olivia," says Katherine. "What kind of dress are you looking for?"

"Oh, I don't know. I'm more of a pant and sweater kind of girl," answers Olivia.

"I'm with you, Olivia," says Brooke. "These girls and their dresses and heels. Who needs to torture themselves like that? I look just as nice and I'm much more comfortable than they are."

"I thought you dressed like that because you're a teacher," says Katherine.

"Yes, but I prefer pants over dresses anyway. I don't know how you and Lydia wear those heels. How can they be comfortable at all?" asks Brooke.

"Well, I can't speak for Lydia, but I like the height they add, me being so short," says Katherine. "I can speak for Isaac, though, he hates them, and says shoes like these are bad for our knees."

"He's right, of course. He's a doctor, but for now I'm going for glam," laughs Lydia. "I buy a new pair, put them way in back of the closet, and bring them out gradually."

"Whoah, look at this mom," says Brigit.

"Whoah is right, maybe you can wear that little number over my dead body," says Alexis.

"Mom, I'm twenty-four years old."

"Yes, and I'm still alive, so put it back," says Alexis. "How about this one?"

"I like it! I'm going to try it on," says Brigit.

"Nava, what do you have there?" asks Malka.

"I have always wanted a red dress. What do you think?" I find a classy red dress, and I hope it fits.

"It's *gorgeous*, Aunt Nava. You *have* to buy it," says Lydia.

"It's not too much?" I ask.

"Sister, you have to at least try it on, it's really beautiful."

"All right then, I'll be back." I make my way to the dressing room. I am led to an available spot and I take off my coat when I hear familiar voices.

"Don't you love Aunt Nava?"

"I do. She's just as mother described her all these years."

"Yes, but too bad she brought –"

"Come on, give her a chance. Like Aunt Nava said, she's been through a lot."

"Haven't we all been through something? None of us act this way. So angry, so hateful. Isaac and Lydia bring her into their home with open arms and she acts like a spoiled brat. She is in her forties and she's acting like she's ten. Enough already! Who needs that kind of negativity? I want to get to know Aunt Nava and to heck with her. I think I'm going to get this dress. I want to find a purse to go with it."

"It looks great on you, let's go."

The dressing room area is now quiet. They must all feel this way. *Oh, Olivia, let them see the real you, before it's too late.*

"That was fun, now what?" asks Alexis.

"Well, it's almost noon, how about some lunch?" asks Lydia.

"That sounds great," said Alexis. Where would you like to go?"

"DeMarco's for sure. I'll call for a reservation, do you have the number?"

"I do, right here in my phone."

"What are you two talking about," asks Malka.

"Lunch, at DeMarco's, is that all right?" asks Lydia.

"Lydia, you know it's my favorite. Of course it's all right. Sister, we're going to DeMarco's for lunch. You're going to love it. It's my favorite Italian restaurant in the city."

"Sounds delicious. Is it far?"

"It's a bit of a drive, but we have plenty of time."

The ride to the restaurant was spent listening to chatter about dresses, shoes, purses and hairstyles. It was music to my ears. These ladies really enjoy spending time together. There is so much love between them, I'm so glad to be a part of it. It sounds trivial, but these ladies have such golden hearts. I could listen to this symphony for hours.

"Here we are," says Lydia. "Shopping makes me hungry!"

"Hello. Howard, party of nine."

"Yes, right this way, your table is ready," said the host.

"You're right Malka, this is lovely." Fine linens, candlelight on the tables, rich decorations with beautiful background music. We are led to a long table, set for nine with four small vases filled with flowers, glowing in the candlelight down the middle of the table.

"It is beautiful, but the food here, that's the best part. You'll see," says Malka.

I open my menu, and my eyes are drawn to 'sweet corn ravioli and lobster'.

Here we are ladies, hope you brought your appetites."

"Yes, of course. Oh, look at this. Just wonderful!" says Malka.

"You were right, sister. This ravioli is melting in my mouth," I smile at my sister, enjoying our moment. "What did you get, Olivia?" She was at the other end of the table with Brooke and Alexis.

"Sweet corn ravioli and lobster," she said. There were chuckles around the table.

"You two are definitely mother and daughter," says Lydia.

"What's that supposed to mean?" asks Olivia.

"It's just an observation, Olivia, calm down. You're at opposite ends of the table and you ordered the same dish. No need to get defensive."

"I'm not getting defensive, just wondering what you meant, is all," says Olivia.

"You know, I've had just about enough of your –"

"What are you having, Alexis?" I smile at her. I need to nip this in the bud.

She smiles back, "I'm having the chianti braised short ribs, Aunt Nava. One of my favorites here."

"Sounds delicious. And you, Brooke? What are you having?"

"The asparagus ravioli," she says with a smile.

"Nicely done, sister," says Malka.

I lean over to her and whisper, "I don't know what to do. I didn't think she would be like this. She seemed open to coming and getting to know your family. Now I feel like there are land mines buried and I'm afraid to step on one."

"Poor sister, have a taste of my lamb chops, it will melt in your mouth."

"Mmmm. I think we may have to come back here again this week, and bring the rest of the family too."

"Anything you want, Nava. I'm so glad you're here in Houston. Maybe you can extend your stay. Maybe another week?"

"Oh, yes, Aunt Nava," says Lydia. "I can call the airline for you and get your ticket changed if you'd like."

"What? What did you say?" asks Olivia.

"Your mother might stay longer. That's okay with you, right Olivia?" asks Brooke.

I glance at Olivia and meet eyes with her. "Nothing has been decided, Olivia, I was just telling your Aunt Malka I was enjoying my stay and she suggested I stay longer, that's all."

"I see," said Olivia. "So it begins," she whispers under her breath.

"So what begins," Brooke shoots back. "What the hell is your problem? Is it your goal in life to ruin every occasion while you're here?"

"Who saved room for dessert?" asks the waiter.

"We all did," says Malka, interrupting the spat. "Warm chocolate ricotta cake for everyone, thank you." The waiter smiles and returns to the kitchen.

"There will be no more of that at this table or any other table during this trip, understood?" Heads bow in embarrassment. Malka takes my hand and smiles. "I'm so glad you're here." We both begin to laugh, just like old times.

30

Nava

"Look at these ladies, Tim," says Isaac. "We are lucky to be surrounded by such beauty."

"They had a good day shopping, I hear," says Tim.

"For the most part, I hear," says Luke. "Apparently there was a little spat at lunch."

"Hush, son," says Malka. "Lunch was lovely, nothing to speak of, really."

"Whatever you say, Mother," says Isaac. "Let's go, the bus is out front waiting."

The bus ride to the museum was eerily quiet, so I enjoyed the view. Busy neighborhoods, cars waiting for lights to change, people on the sidewalks walking quickly in the chilly weather.

"Nava? … Nava?" says Malka.

"Yes? Oh, sorry. Just watching the busyness of the streets, I guess."

"We're here, are you ready?"

"Yes, of course," I say and take her hand.

The moment I walk through the doors I could feel it. The heaviness, as though someone threw a blanket over me. My steps become slow and heavy.

"Mom?" says Olivia. "This way."

"Yes, I'm coming." I follow Olivia into the main foyer, I look all around me.

"Are you all right?" asks Malka. "This is a very special place, I spend a lot of time here.

"Yes, I'm fine," I say, but I can still feel my heavy heart and I make more of an effort to lift my heavy feet. *Put a smile on your face. Just be here for Malka, the rest will be fine.*

There are a lot of people waiting. I quickly realized they are waiting for my sister.

"Good evening everyone, my name is Malka Prinz-Howard and I am pleased to welcome you to the Holocaust Museum of Houston. Do we have anyone here visiting Houston from out of town?" Several hands go up. "Wonderful, I'm so glad you made this museum one of your stops. I hope everyone from near and far realize what a special place this is. I spend a lot of time here, as does my very supportive family."

"I myself am a survivor of the Holocaust," she continues. I was fourteen years old when I arrived at Auschwitz, and I was there for about three and a half years before I was transferred to another camp. I was devastated by this transfer. My twin sister was at Auschwitz as well, and until recently, I had no idea what happened to her. This is my sister, Nava. Sister, please come join me for a moment."

The crowd applauds as I join my sister. She takes my hand and smiles. "We were apart for so long, and now we're together again. It is a true miracle." There is more applause. "Thank you, thank you so much."

"We are here tonight to share with you the Museum's permanent exhibit, called "Bearing Witness: A Community Remembers'. You will see authentic film footage, artifacts, photographs and documents that show life in pre-war Europe, continuing with the Nazi's Final Solution and then life after the Holocaust. The Permanent Exhibit ends with a short film called "Voices." This is a wonderful film which I am so proud to be a part of. Survivors in the Houston area have come together to share our experiences."

"You will also see an authentic 1942 World War II railcar and a 1942 Danish fishing boat used to save more than 7,200 Danish Jews from certain death. Please take your time, take it all in. Some of what you see may be difficult to watch, but remember, it was even more difficult to live through – we are lucky we lived through it, as so many did not. Let's begin." Walking down the corridor I can hear people talking behind me. Some are shocked at what they're seeing, expressing empathy and disbelief that this happened, this thing known as the

Holocaust.

I came upon a striped uniform. I couldn't touch the fabric, it is behind glass, but I stand there and stare at it. The faded stripes, the crooked stitching, the yellow star. Patches at the knees. How many people wore this uniform? It is tiny but it was made for a man. A *man.* I close my eyes and I can see the sonderkommander I spoke to a few times, skin and bones. A starving body could fit into such a small uniform. I try to stop a tear from falling, but it is too late.

"Mother, this is too much for you, maybe we should go," says Olivia.

"Absolutely not. I am right where I need to be. Olivia, look at this uniform. Look at how small it is – a grown man wore that uniform. Probably hundreds wore it, maybe thousands. And here it is in this Museum, for everyone to see. They look at this and keep walking. They look at it but don't *see* it. They don't know who wore this uniform. They don't know what he went through. To them it's an old striped uniform, faded from wear and tear and time. Look at it, Olivia. *See* it. Understand what that uniform means." We stand there in silence for several minutes. I look up at Olivia. There are tears on her cheeks now. "Should we go? Is it too much for you?" I ask her.

"Absolutely not," she says. I take her hand and we keep walking.

I am mesmerized by the photographs, the videos. I am watching a video when Malka appears at my side. "Come with me sister, there is something you have to do."

"Oh? All right, where are we going?"

"Just come with me," she says. "Olivia, we'll be back with you in a little while."

We walk quite a distance, and while we walk we chat a little bit. "This is a special place, so much work to bring all of these things together for people to see," I say, taking her arm.

"Yes, it's a wonderful tribute, Nava." She stops and turns to face me. "Sister, I need you to trust me now. This is for your own good, all right?"

"All right. Malka, you're acting so strangely, what's the matter?" I am trying to read her eyes, and then I see it. "*No, Malka.*"

"Yes, sister. You must. Take my hand, you'll be all right," she says. "Come with me. Trust me, Nava."

"No, not this. Not even for you, Malka. I won't do it!" I turn to leave, but she grabs my shoulders.

"Nava, come with me. You need this. I'm right here with you, you'll be fine. Here, take my hand."

I step onto the rail car behind Malka. "I can't breathe, sister, I can't breathe!"

"Yes, Nava. You can breathe. Breathe with me, nice and slow. Nava ... breathe, honey. It's okay ... it's okay." We stand there in each other's arms, breathing together, crying together. "Come, Nava. Walk with me. It's just the two of us. Look, plenty of room. Look, Nava. The train isn't moving. It's just you and me."

She was right, it wasn't moving, and it wasn't full of scared, unknowing people. "Right here," I said. "I stood right here, against Mother. She was holding Isaak, and you were right here."

"Yes, we were right here, together," says Malka. "And here we are again, in this spot, but we're okay, Nava. We're all right. Right? Let it out, Nava. You have kept it all in for so long. Aren't you tired, sweetheart? Tired of holding it all in? Let it out, Nava. Let it *go*."

I have never cried so hard and for so long in my life – not even when William died. This was different; this was all the guilt, all the shame, all the heartache flowing outside of me. All the pain, the hunger, the lukewarm soup and moldy bread, the cold coffee; the piles of naked bodies, the barking dogs, the screaming soldiers, the whistle of the trains, the gray snow, the roll calls, the striped dress, and the shoes that didn't fit. It all came out, all of it.

I felt Malka's hands on my face. "There she is," she says. "There's my Nava."

31

Tim

She stands at the glass, watching the video, the full loop, and then she moves on to the next one and watches that video. She walks very slowly, looking at every photograph, listens to everything she can. To look at her, she is in a trance. Sometimes she raises her right hand and touches the glass; sometimes she raises it to touch her face. If you watch her closely you would notice she doesn't blink for a long time. She is mesmerized by it all. Every so often another tear makes its way down her cheek.

It all sinks in, the experience. The uniforms, the trains, the soldiers, the barracks, the gas chambers, the piles of the dead. It absorbs her like a sponge, the words, the pictures, the countless black and white faces.

She can sense I am beside her but she doesn't turn to look at me. "She lived through all of this, Tim. She went through all of this. They both did."

I put my arm around her. "Yes, they did, and they survived it," I say.

"How?" She turns to me, her face tear-stained and pale. "How did they get out of that alive?"

"I don't know, sweetheart, I don't know." I rub her back, relaxing her.

"Mom, are you okay?" asks Alex.

"She's fine son, just a lot to take in," I tell him.

"Where's Grandma and Malka?" asks Abbie.

"I'm not sure," says Olivia. "Malka took her somewhere to show her something." She glances at her watch. That was quite a while ago. Maybe we should go look for them."

"No," I say.

"No? Why not?" asks Olivia.

"Because they're fine. We're here with you now. Are you fine?" I ask her.

"I'm okay. Like you said, it's a lot to take in." She looks back at the glass at some photographs.

"What are you thinking right now, Liv?" I persist. "What's on your mind?"

"I'm the child of a survivor. I never really understood what that meant until now. I get it. I get it now."

"What do you get, Liv?" I need to hear the words.

"Why she did it, why she came here to America. Why she wanted to start over as a completely different person. Why she kept her secrets for so long. I don't know how to explain it, I just … get it."

I smile at her, relieved, knowing she had to come to this on her own, in her own time. The past few weeks have been hard for her, but now things would be different. I have been with her long enough to know how to handle her, how to have the right amount of patience. Looking at her now I can see my 'Liv' has come back. The softness in her face has returned, the tension lines in her forehead and cheeks have vanished.

"What are you smiling at?" she asks me.

"My beautiful wife, that's who," I say.

"I'm sorry, Tim. I've been such a nightmare –"

"No, you've been you," I laugh.

"Thanks a lot!" she laughs back, fake punching me in the arm.

"I know you, Liv. I knew you would come around when you were ready. Coming here, to this place. It's what you needed, what we all needed, to understand. Am I right?"

"Yes, you're right," she says. "I feel so foolish. How I've been acting – towards Mother. And Malka and her family, I'm so embarrassed."

"There's really no need," says Isaac from behind us. He is standing with his family, smiling at us.

"Oh, Isaac," says Olivia, walking into his embrace. "You're my cousin, not my enemy. I'm so sorry I took so long to realize that."

"It's okay, really," he says. "I understand where you're coming from."

She looks up and sees the whole family there. "Oh, gosh. What you all must think of me…"

"We just thought you were a typical New Yorker!" says Brooke, and laughter breaks the tension.

"Maybe so," says Olivia. "Maybe so."

"Group hug, everybody … come on, everyone in," says Luke. Maybe this extended family isn't so bad after all.

"Well, what's going on here?" asks Malka. She has Nava with her.

"Oh, Aunt Malka," says Olivia. "Please forgive me."

"Nonsense, come here," says Malka, embracing her.

"Mother," says Olivia, taking Nava's hands. "I *saw* it. I really saw *everything*. I can't believe it, I can't believe all that you lived through. You were both so young. I understand now, I get it."

"Get what, sweetheart?" asks Nava with a smile.

"Why you came here, why you wanted to start a new life. Wait," says Olivia. "Are you all right? You're all pale, like you've been crying."

"I have had an understanding of my own, Olivia. An awakening, so to speak."

"What happened?" asks Olivia.

"Your Aunt Nava knew what I needed. All these years, bottling everything inside, it was just too much. She knew that, even better than I did."

"So what happened?" asks Abbie.

"I, well, she brought me inside the rail car," says Nava.

"What? Malka, don't you think –"

"What I think, Olivia, is she needed to experience that this way, instead of through her memory, her awful memories of a rail car," says Malka. "It was only the two of us, and she knew she was safe. She let years and years of pain go, they were washed away. It's exactly what she needed."

"Oh, Mother," says Olivia. "Do you really feel better?"

"I do, I just feel exhausted. Don't look so worried, I'm fine," says Nava. "Malka was right, she really was. She would never do anything to hurt me, Olivia."

"I know that, Mother. Things are happening so fast, you've been upset, we've all been getting used to everything. I don't want any set-backs

"Well, let's get going, so you can get some rest," I say.

"Grandma, I saw a lot of things here," says Abbie. "Can I tell you something?"

"Of course Abbie, go ahead."

"Some of it made me cry, because that happened to you. You were there."

"I'm sorry, Grandma," says Alex.

"Please, don't apologize. Let's go home," says Nava, taking their hands.

"Home to New York?" asks Abbie.

"To New York, at the end of the week. To our Houston home for now."

"You are coming back to New York with us though, right?" asks Abbie.

"Yes, I'm going back to New York with you, but I'll be coming back to Houston real soon."

"Well that's music to my ears," says Malka. You come and visit as often as you want. And don't think I won't be using that spare room at the penthouse."

"It's not a spare room, Malka. It's *your* room now. Anytime you want to use it."

"I know you're tired, but how about we all go for a quick dessert at DeMarco's?"

"That sounds like a great way to end the night," says Lydia.

32

Nava

As I walk into the dining room for dinner with my family, I can't help but notice how beautiful the table looks. "Lydia, this is just beautiful!"

"Oh, thanks Aunt Nava," says Lydia. "There's just something about a set table that I just love."

"She thinks it makes the food taste better," laughs Isaac.

"Very funny. Don't listen to him, Aunt Nava," says Lydia. "He never complains about my cooking, and he better not start now."

"Come on now, sweetie," says Isaac, pulling Lydia into his arms. "You know I'm kidding, and you know I think you're amazing."

"Well, thank you. That's better," she says, and gives him a quick kiss.

Nina places a salad bowl in front of me. "Thank you, Nina." I can't help but stare at it. It is a small, round wooden bowl. The vibrant vegetables become black and white. "Move along!" An SS officer is glaring at me as I continue walking with my bowl of lukewarm 'soup'. It is raining and my ill-fitting clogs keep getting stuck in the mud, slowing me down.

"Mother? Mother, do you not want salad?" asks Olivia, and I come out of my daydream. Everyone is looking at me.

"Oh yes, I love salad," I say. I can feel myself shaking.

"Where were you just then?" asks Olivia.

"I'm right here. I'm fine," I say, trying to sound convincing.

"It's the bowl," says Malka. I look up at her and quickly shake my head, hoping this will make her stop. "It's the bowl and she's fine."

"I don't understand," says Lydia. "Would you like a different

115

bowl, Aunt Nava?"

"What's going on?" asks Olivia.

"Everyone, please. I'm fine," I plead.

"In Auschwitz we used bowls like these," says Malka. "We guarded them with our lives. We carried them everywhere because you didn't get another one if you lost it or if someone stole it. It's all we had to eat from and often times they were used for a toilet as well."

"Oh, God," says Lydia. She stands up. "Nina help me. Let's get these bowls out of here. I am so sorry, Aunt Nava, I had no idea. Hurry Nina. Please."

"Nina, stay right where you are. Lydia, please sit down." She walks over to me. "Nava, this is a wooden bowl, but it's not *that* bowl. Okay?" She puts her hand on my shoulder and gives it a loving squeeze.

"Okay," I say. "Okay." I look at her and calmness comes over me like a fuzzy blanket. She smiles at me and walks back to her seat.

"Let's eat," says Malka, and takes a sip of her tea.

"Um, what just happened here?" asks Olivia.

"She's fine, Olivia. She has post-traumatic stress. She has hidden her feelings so long, everything is a trigger, and everything will be until we do something about it."

"And what are we doing about it?" asks Olivia. "Mother, I don't know what to say."

"Olivia, I have convinced your mother to speak to someone, he's coming to the house to talk with her. Tomorrow."

"Really? Mother, I'm speechless. I'm so proud of you, agreeing to talk to someone," says Olivia.

"I'm so embarrassed," I say.

An orchestra of "Don't be silly," "It's a great thing to do," and "Don't feel that way," fills the room.

"Aunt Nava, we're all here for you, and we'll do anything and everything to help you through this process," says Isaac.

"Amen to that," says Malka. "Let's eat. This all looks wonderful."

33

Nava

Today is my first session with Dr. Nick, as he likes to be called. I am very nervous, but also grateful that Malka is having him see me at Isaac and Lydia's home for our sessions.

"Nava, I'm so nervous," I confide in her. "What if I can't do it, what if I can't talk about my past?"

"You repressed everything for so long, Nava. It all needs to be released, almost like a cleansing. That's when you will come alive again."

"I'm not dead, sister," I say.

"Of course you're not, but you'll see. The more you talk to Dr. Nick the more of a difference you'll see in yourself. It happened to me, and it will happen for you too."

"I hope you're right," I say.

"Look at that photograph over there, Nava. Look at our parents, and look at me and look at you. Our parents and Isaak, they're gone. You and I, we're still here, and we're going to be just fine. Look at you! You escaped death, *twice*! You're stronger than you think."

"If you don't mind, I'm going to lay down for a bit," I say and walk into my room. Malka is in our sitting area in the suite.

"Sure, I'll see you later," she says, and continues to read her book.

I lie down and pull the afghan over me. It feels so good to lie down and close my eyes for a while.

You! You! And you! I said eyes front not eyes closed! You want to rest? You will rest! One by one the soldier shoots all three men, right in the forehead. Their crime was closing their eyes during morning count. We had been standing there for hours. It was early in the morning, still dark out. Who would have known closing your eyes was punishable by death. But that's how it was in Auschwitz; the only people punished were the living skeletons in striped uniforms.

"Aunt Nava? Aunt Nava, wake up, you're dreaming," says Katherine.

"Oh, Katherine. What time is it?" I ask.

"It's almost two," she says and helps me sit up. "Feel up to a walk?"

"How nice, I'll be ready in just a minute," I say and put my boots on.

Katherine is right; it is a beautiful day for a walk. I am able to increase my pace a little bit and pay careful attention to my breathing. When we return, we are greeted with hot chocolate and cookies.

"Sugar-free hot chocolate and gluten free cookies. Doctor's orders," says Nina.

"Dr. Lydia?" asks Katherine with a chuckle.

"Yes, that's right. She has bought some new cookbooks and this is a new cookie recipe. I hope you like it."

"Thank you, Nina. I'm going to love it, I promise," I say. Lydia is so thoughtful, Malka is right, she's a dream.

Just then the doorbell rings. "That must be Dr. Nick. He's very punctual, I'll give him that," says Katherine.

"Hello, Dr. Nick," says Lydia as she opens the door and invites him in.

"Thank you, Lydia. Nava, nice to meet you. You've got pink cheeks, have you been outside?" asks Dr. Nick.

"Yes, Katherine and I just came in from a walk," I say. Dr. Nick is a friend of the family, and he also sees Malka as a patient. She trusts him implicitly and is confident he can help me.

"Are you up for our session?" he asks as he hands Nina his coat.

"Yes, of course," I say, though I'm still a little nervous about talking about my past.

"Is there a private spot where we can talk?" he asks.

"Yes, come on in." I take him into the library, and we sit

down.

"You look a little anxious," says Dr. Nick. "I hope you will begin to feel comfortable with me as our meetings progress. I will tell you that all the years I have met with Malka there hasn't been a single session when she didn't talk about you. I feel like I already know you, to some extent."

"I can only imagine what she said. I hope my sister didn't fill your head with fables," I say. "She tends to exaggerate." We both laugh. His laugh and his eyes remind me of Dr. Krane, they both have very kind eyes.

"Tell me about your life this past year. I understand you lost your husband," he says.

I shift in my chair. *He gets right to it, doesn't he?* "Yes, I lost William about a year ago now."

"How long were you married?" asks Dr. Nick.

"We were married over fifty years," I say. "I miss him so."

Dr. Nick smiles and nods, and writes something on his pad of paper. "Since his passing, you have been experiencing some memory recall, is that right?"

"Yes, that's right," I say. "The images, they are so vivid."

"Are you awake when you see these images?" he asks.

"I have dreams, yes. I had a dream today, actually."

"Today?" he asks, intrigued.

"Well ... I took a nap earlier, and I had a dream. I was at Auschwitz, it was dark and we were standing outside for morning count. All of a sudden a soldier picked out three prisoners and screamed at them. Apparently, they had closed their eyes. For that they were shot, in the forehead. The things I saw there, I just can't –"

"You saw things no one should ever have to see. On top of that you were a young girl, a teenager."

"Yes, and I learned very quickly that my life could end at any moment, for any reason. People died – so many people – for closing their eyes, for walking too slow, for standing in the wrong spot, for no reason at all. Just because we were there, because we were Jewish, because they could do anything they wanted, they had no consequences, no conscience, and no remorse. I will never understand it."

"Understand what?" asks Dr. Nick.

"How they got away with it for so many years. It was just accepted, the way it was. No one said anything. You couldn't say anything, you couldn't help anyone, and you couldn't talk back. If you did you were shot. We all tried to do what we were told, quickly, to not look any soldiers in the eye, to not draw any attention to ourselves."

"Your survival, your sister's survival, they're miracles, you know that don't you?"

"I know. We are also lucky we were not identical twins. Who knows what would have happened if we were. We wouldn't be here today, that's for certain."

"I have read, quite extensively, about Dr. Mengele."

"The angel of death, he was called," I said. "He stood right there when another train would arrive, looking intently for twins. I had been there for quite a while before I even heard his name and the things that he did. I thank God every night for my sister and for not making her look just like me. It saved our lives, I'm sure of it."

"What did you know of your sister while you were at the camp, were you able to stay close to one another?" asks Dr. Nick.

"No, not really," I say.

"Nava, do you not want to talk about this?" he asks.

"Not really," I say. I shift in my seat again. I can feel my face getting warm.

"I think it would help you, will you give it a try?"

"I don't think so," I say.

"Would it help if she were here with you? We can ask her to join us if you'd like."

"I ... I don't know. Maybe it would help. Maybe I'll just have a cup of tea, would you like some?" I pour my tea and look at Dr. Nick for his answer.

"No, thank you. You go ahead."

I nod and take a sip of tea.

"Shall I get your sister, Nava?" asks Dr. Nick.

"No, not today," I say. "Maybe next time."

"We still have ten more minutes, but if you'd like to stop for today, that's okay with me," says Dr. Nick.

"Maybe we should stop, for today." I can't help but feel relieved.

"Okay, that's fine," he says, standing up. "Are we still on for Friday?"

"Yes, Friday. I'll walk you out." We walk into the foyer and I hand Dr. Nick his coat.

"Done so soon?" asks Malka as she walks down the staircase.

"Done for today, yes. I'll be back on Friday. I'll see you then. Good work today, Nava," says Dr. Nick as he walks out the door.

"Thank you, I'll see you on Friday," I say as I close the front door.

The door was barely closed when Malka asks, "What was that all about?"

"What do you mean?" I ask. I try to walk by her to go upstairs.

She steps in my path. "Why did your session end early?"

"Ten minutes, Malka. Ten minutes early."

"Yes, and I want to know why." She's getting impatient with me.

"We were at a good stopping point, that's all. He'll be back in a couple days. I don't know why you're making such a big deal over ten minutes." I try to walk past her, but again, she blocks my path.

"I want you to get better, that's all. Taking to him will make you better, if you would just talk to him."

"I am talking to him. You are so pushy, Malka, just like when we were younger!"

"And you are closed-off and guarded, just like when we were younger!" she shot back.

"Hey, what's going on in here?" says Katherine, running into

121

the room. "This is not good, for either of you."

"Butt out, Katherine," snaps Malka. "If I want to yell at my sister, I will thank you very much."

"You will *not* yell at your sister and undo all the progress we've made. And I will *not* butt out. I've never even heard you say that, what are you watching MTV now?"

That was all she needed to say to break the tension. Malka and I look at each other and start to laugh, almost uncontrollably. I laugh so hard I start to cry, and I have to say, it feels *so good*.

34

Olivia

Mother, Malka, Dr. Nick and I are all in the library together. Dr. Nick thinks it would be beneficial for Mother to answer all my questions in this intimate environment. There are so many questions I want to ask her, so I'm excited for this session.

"Olivia, I want to help you understand your mother and her past and why she kept her past a secret for so long," says Dr. Nick. "I want to help Nava feel comfortable in opening up about her past, and of course Malka is here for support and maybe fill in a few blanks if need be. How does that sound for everyone?"

"That sounds great," I say. "I want to know everything." I see Mother take a deep breath. She's nervous and knows my questions will be difficult. "Start from the beginning."

My mother is staring at me and words do not come. I look at Dr. Nick, and he says to Mother, "Take your time, Nava. No one is going to rush you. You tell your story."

I continue to stare and at her, trying to will the words to come out. She takes another sip of tea. She puts her hand on her wrist and slowly pulls up the sleeve to her sweater. My eyes fall to her arm, watching. Slowly, the numbers are revealed. She stops. She is looking at me and I am looking at her arm. My eyes move upward and we are looking at each other. It is as though I suddenly see her, the inside of her.

"Oh, Mother," I say. She says nothing. Our eyes meet again, and a single tear rolls down her cheek. I pull her arm towards me and start to rub her arm with a single finger. I lean down and kiss her arm. If only that would erase it. Of course, it doesn't.

For what seems like hours, we just sit there in silence. I am rubbing her arm, I am watching her, letting her take her time to begin her story.

"I know you have questions." She surprises me by breaking the silence first.

"Yes, I do. Are you ready to answer them?" I ask. I look at her, almost begging her to say yes. Then I remember.

"Olivia?" says Dr. Nick.

"I am a fool. I am so sorry," I say.

"For what?" asks Mother.

"When Abbie and I were at the penthouse, your reaction to seeing the DVD she had with her. *Schindler's List.* I will never forget the look on your face, it says it all."

"How could you have known? Why would you question my reaction?"

"I wish I had known. I thought we were Catholic."

"Your father was Catholic, and you were brought up Catholic."

"All these years, I thought I knew everything about you. Everything! I don't know anything at all, do I."

"That's my fault, not yours," says Mother. "Coming to America was a journey I took to reinvent myself. I came here to New York with the dream of becoming something more than a survivor. I was alone, my family was gone, or so I thought. The opportunity came to come here so I did. Many survivors came here."

"Mother, I want to know you. *All* of you," I say. "I am here and I'm listening. I don't care how long this takes. I'm not going anywhere. I promise." I look at Malka and Dr. Nick.

"Nava, we have all the time you need," says Dr. Nick. "I think the beginning would be a good place to start."

I look at my sister, who takes my hand and smiles at me. She gives me a quick nod.

I take a deep breath, and another sip of tea. Slowly, I begin. "The beginning. Well, I was born in Czechoslovakia. I mean, *we* were born in Czechoslovakia. Our father owned his own business, an accounting firm. It was on the ground floor of our building. There was a large window with fancy white printing, "Jakob H. Prinz and Associates." There were hanging plants in the window. It was my job to water them every day after school. Malka's job was to sweep the floors." Malka gives my hand a little squeeze. She is smiling at me, and I know she remembers this as well. "Along the left side of the wall were three desks, all facing the big window. These desks were for the "associates." I remember watching them – their left hand on papers, their right hand quickly grazing the buttons of their adding machines. Way in the back was Father's office. It was enclosed with a glass door with his name on it. On his desk was a beautiful photograph of my mother. She looked like a movie star. There were no photos of me, or Malka, but on the wall to his right were some drawings we did for him at school. He told me he loved these drawings and showed them to everyone who came in to see him. That made me so happy."

"He was so proud of those silly drawings," chuckles Malka.

"On the second floor was our apartment. When you walked in there was our dining table. There was always a vase full of flowers on it, sitting on a white lace table runner that my great-grandmother had made. It was old and delicate but very beautiful. We were always careful not to spill anything on our mother's favorite heirloom."

"To the left was our living room. There was a sofa and two large comfy chairs separated by a small table with a lamp and a stack of books on it. My love of reading comes from them. Malka shares that love too. Our parents always sat in those chairs. They would read, or talk, or listen to us tell them about our day. We were a very close family and enjoyed each other's company."

"I was a very lucky girl – I had my own bedroom, with fancy bed covers. I had many dolls and games to play with. There was a desk for me to do my homework on or write letters to our cousins, Hannah and Silvie. They lived in Berlin."

"My mother worked at home, her job was to take care of us and keep our home clean and beautiful. Sometimes she would help our father downstairs when we were at school."

"We had many friends and I had a wonderful childhood. Our

picture-perfect life lasted until we were twelve years old."

"What happened then?" I ask her.

"Well, Mother announced she was having a baby. I was twelve years old! I didn't want a baby brother or sister so much younger than me. I later learned that my mother miscarried many babies. We would have had three other siblings! I had no idea, but realized that is why she was so excited about this baby. Eventually, I was excited too."

"Things started to change quickly, not because of the baby, but because things became political. It became very difficult to be a Jewish person where we lived. All over Europe, really. Jews were not allowed to own a business, or even work. Our father was forced to close his business. He didn't say much but we knew he was heartbroken. Jewish kids could no longer attend school. Our friends who were not Jewish would have nothing to do with us. There were curfews and food rationing. It was awful. We stayed inside our apartment all the time. The streets were full of soldiers, Jews had to wear a yellow star on all of their clothing at all times. There were random beatings and even shootings right in the streets, right in front of everyone."

"In the mail one day we received a postcard. It was asking for volunteers to go work in a factory. It promised work, it promised a better life, and most importantly is promised us a way out of our town that had changed so much. We left just a couple days later. We were allowed to bring one suitcase each. We were on a passenger train and we didn't even know where we were going, but we thought we were going somewhere better than where we were."

"We were on that train for about twelve hours or so, and then it stopped at a station. We were then transferred to another train, this one not so nice. My mother said, "There must be some mistake. That's a cattle car." We were told to get into it, with all the others. There must have been 70 of us, maybe more, crammed in this little cattle car. There were no seats, of course, so we all stood, pinned against each other. We stood like that for two days."

"I can't even imagine what that was like, Mother," I say. I let go of her arm and rest my face in my hands. I am trying to let it all sink in, my poor mother's childhood.

"Nava, can you continue?" asks Dr. Nick. "We can take a break if you'd like."

Mother takes a breath and slowly shakes her head. She's going to keep going.

"I closed my eyes to try to block out the chatter around me. Complaining, mostly. Sore feet, exhaustion, hunger, someone stepped on another's foot. It went on and on. I would exchange glances with my mother and my sister, but we said nothing. What good would it do, anyway?"

"There were cracks, or small openings, in the cattle car. We could see through them – small slices of time passing us by."

"Suddenly, there was light coming through the cracks in the cattle car. Not sunlight, but bright, blinding lights. The whistle of the train sounded, over and over, and the train came to a stop. The door opened, and we were all rushed out. There were wooden ramps, and we hurried down them. There were many buildings, and I could see one with a tall chimney and the smoke just poured out of it. There were flecks of something in the air, it looked like snow, but how could that be, it was August. There were dogs barking, huge German Shepherds, and soldiers that looked to be larger than life. Faces of stone and dark uniforms. I was so scared."

"Isaak, he started to cry – of all times to start crying."

"Malka told us, Mother. About your brother and how he died," I say. "In the waiting room at the hospital. She told us about Isaak."

She looks at me and nods. "Olivia, I have not spoken of these things in years! I can still see her, my mother, walking away, the last time I ever saw her." She wipes her face and sips more tea. I hold her hand, still stroking the numbers. Tears roll down my face, but through my tears I see her; really see her. I am not angry, and I look at her, silently pleading with her to continue.

"We were led to a stairway that went underground. There was a large area, hooks lining the walls, and there were benches. We were told to remove all of our clothing and hang them on the hooks, then go into another room for a shower. Briefly, the lights went out, and in that brief moment there were screams in the darkness. The lights came back on, and water came out of the shower heads. Cold water, but water nonetheless. We were given striped working dresses. Faded black and gray striped dresses. The lightest color I saw were the faces of the people there. We were all very pale. My dress was too big for me and my shoes were too small."

"We were taken to another area where they were shaving everyone's heads. For me, this was so upsetting. I loved my long, dark hair. We were told it was because of lice. I didn't have lice, but no one said a word. Compliance meant survival, any backtalk or questioning or resistance got you a beating or even killed. So there I sat, watching my hair fall to the floor. I looked across from me and there was a girl looking right at me. "It will grow back," she said. I nodded. In a place like this, I still worried about my hair. Foolish girl."

I squeeze her hand, gently, and think of all the times I asked my mother to get a haircut. She would always insist I was beautiful just the way I was. I still have long hair to this day. One of the many things that happened throughout my childhood that didn't make sense to me at the time, but now makes perfect sense.

"How do you feel, Nava?" asks Dr. Nick.

"I feel okay," says Mother. "I feel very tired, to be honest."

"You did great, honey," says Malka. "I'm so proud of you."

"There is much more to this story, but I would like to stop for now if that's all right," says Mother. Although I could sit here and listen to her forever, I know that she needs rest. She looks both emotionally and physically drained so I don't press.

"We can continue tomorrow," says Dr. Nick. "I would like to keep going, Nava, in this setting, which means Olivia, outside of this setting no questions. Your mother feels safe telling her story in this manner, so we should proceed accordingly."

"Of course," I say. "I'm just so grateful, that she is letting me in, finally. Thank you, Mother, for sharing all this with me."

Mother and Malka stand up. They excuse themselves to go upstairs and take a nap. I am left in the library with Dr. Nick. "You got a lot of information here today, Olivia," says Dr. Nick. "What do you think of what you learned?"

"I am fascinated to hear of her childhood, of course, but I got some answers to questions I didn't even ask," I say.

"What, for example?" asks Dr. Nick.

"Long hair, for one," I say. "I remember asking her to get a haircut every so often. She would always say no, saying I was beautiful the way I was."

"Isn't that something," says Dr. Nick. "Anything else?"

"We never had showers in our home," I say.

"No showers?" asks Dr. Nick. "Now that's really intriguing, isn't it?"

"I always took baths," I say. "The first time I took a shower, I was in middle school at the end of gym class. My best friend had to show me how to use it!" I laugh.

"I think you're going to learn as much about yourself through this process," says Dr. Nick.

"I think so, too," I say, and walk him to the front door.

35

Nava

We are all back in the library together. Dr. Nick is sitting in a chair, Malka and I are on a small sofa, and Olivia is in a chair opposite Dr. Nick. I am less nervous this session, and Olivia has kept her word – no questions between sessions. I am grateful for her patience and her understanding.

"Nava, if you remember, yesterday we ended the session with you talking about getting your head shaved," says Dr. Nick.

"Yes, I remember," I say. *How could I forget?*

"After you and Malka left the room, Olivia brought up something interesting. She mentioned that throughout her adolescent and teenage years she would ask you to get a haircut, and you would tell her she was beautiful the way she was," says Dr. Nick.

"She has always been beautiful, and she still is," I say.

"Olivia, do you have a question for your mother about that?" asks Dr. Nick.

"Well, I was wondering if one had to do with the other. Me always having long hair and you having your head shaved as a teenager," says Olivia.

I look around the room, and then at my sister, who smiles at me. "Yes, it does," I say. "Of course it does."

"Olivia also mentioned to me that there were never showers in the home," says Dr. Nick. "That's not a coincidence, is it."

"No," I say. "It's not a coincidence. There are things that I would not and could not have in the home. William always supported me in my wishes without question, though I'm sure he knew my reasons."

"He never asked?" asks Olivia.

"No, he never did. Your father and I had an understanding,

Olivia. He granted any wish I had without question, it was just the way he took care of me."

"But he never talked about it with you? Your past?" asks Olivia.

"As I've told you before, he really didn't, Olivia," I say. "He never wanted to know the details. That's what he told me. He said it would break his heart." Malka takes my hand in hers, and gives it a little pat.

"Joshua and I talked about it sometimes," says Malka. "He didn't want to know a lot of details either, but he knew. He was a doctor overseas, that's where we met, so he knew a lot of what went on at the camps through treating me and a lot of other patients."

"There was also another thing I wouldn't allow in the home," I say. "Olivia always wanted a puppy, and I really wish I could have given her one, but it's hard for me, to hear a dog bark. We never took the subway, we never left food on the plate; I always had more than enough food in the house. I still do."

"So you would never be hungry again," says Malka. "I am the exact same way."

"Then there was this." I stroked my arm where the tattoo was. "Those putting them on weren't exactly gentle, they had a job to do, and there were so many to get done. It quickly became red and infected. It was so painful, and it oozed a lot. I never had it treated, I didn't want to go see a doctor about it. I didn't want to draw attention to myself. Here in America, I wore clothes to cover it. That wasn't always easy."

"I imagine that could be quite challenging, sister," says Malka. "Especially in hot weather."

"It was tricky sometimes, but I managed," I said.

"Other questions, Olivia?" asks Dr. Nick.

"Well, maybe the living conditions at the camp. Where did you sleep?"

"Our barracks were full of wooden bunks, no mattresses, sheets or blankets, just bare wood. Three of us had to sleep in each bunk, some even had four people on it. I didn't get a lot of sleep, it was uncomfortable trying to sleep on a board with three other people, and then there was the noise. All through the night you could hear people coughing, some vomiting. There was sickness everywhere. I prayed I would escape it, I wanted to keep my job at Kanada."

"Kanada?" asks Olivia.

"Shortly after I arrived at Auschwitz, I was given a work assignment. After a cup of what they called coffee and a small piece of bread I was taken to a large building with several others, all females. There, we sorted through all kinds of things – shoes, eye glasses, gold fillings, clothing, coats, jewelry, watches, candles, books, instruments, gold, silver and photographs. Many and loose diamonds and other valuables were put in a locked box in the center of the room. We did this until early evening I guess, and then we were led back to the courtyard with everyone else for evening count. This lasted for hours. We were then given a cup of broth and another piece of bread."

"Kanada was a great job to get at the camp. You were lucky, Nava," says Malka. "In the grand scheme of things, anyway. I was in a sewing room, repairing uniforms. The work wasn't so hard, but it was long hours, and I stuck myself with a needle countless times."

"I remember vividly being in line for soup and a sonderkommander seeing my face as I looked at the chimney. He looked me right in the eye and said 'That's your family. That's my family, too.' That moment changed me forever," I say.

"Sonder –" says Olivia.

"Sonderkommander," says Malka. "Oh, the SS were a sadistic group. What better way to further degrade someone than to make them do the dirty work before they too were eventually sent to the gas chamber. They were divided into several groups, each having a specific job. Some greeted new arrivals and told them they needed to be disinfected and showered before being sent to work teams. These were the only sonderkommanders to have contact with victims while they were still alive. Other teams processed corpses. They would remove gold teeth before taking them to the crematorium."

"I asked him, 'Do you ever tell them they are going to be killed?' and he said 'What would be the point? They were defenseless, why frighten them for no good reason?' But his friend said that he told them the truth, and even where to be in the gas chamber so they would die immediately without suffering. To be in such a position, I cannot imagine."

"I can't imagine it either," says Olivia. My daughter has a good heart. I worry she will never get these visions out of her head.

"Maybe I should stop, Olivia. You're getting upset and there is no need for you to keep these stories inside you. Let's stop now."

"Mother, I said I wanted to know all of you and I truly meant it. Please, this means so much to me. Tell me more about the sonderkommanders."

"Well, they went through selection like everyone else. Every new arrival was put in rows of five, and in front of everyone stood soldiers along with doctors. The soldier would point at every person individually and then point to either the left or the right. The left meant death, the right meant work until death."

"Sonderkommanders did horrible work, but they had decent food, slept on straw mattresses and could wear regular clothing. However, they only had these jobs for a few months and they were gassed right along with the others. I myself would see these men, eating and drinking amongst the corpses and I thought, 'How awful, to become so indifferent and so detached that to eat and drink next to a pile of dead bodies was normal.' The truth is, we all functioned this way. We were robots, all of us, and it was how we survived, how we got through another day alive. There was nothing we could do for those corpses, they were already gone. We were still there. We all knew that we could be in one of those piles at any moment."

"Mother, this may seem like a strange question, but I'm curious. Did you meet any friends there? You must have talked to someone."

"There were a few women who were near me working, and yes, we would talk to each other a little bit. There was one woman there in particular that I remember fondly. Her name was Greta and she was beautiful. I think she was older than me, twenty maybe. Even with a shaved head she was stunning. Big, beautiful eyes and a perfect oval face."

"Where was she from?"

"She was from Poland. Every morning I would look for her at morning count and when I spotted her, I felt better, like I would survive another day. That probably sounds strange to you, amidst all the goings on of this camp, but that's how I felt. I was just a girl. I didn't see Malka everyday, only so often, but Greta, she was a constant after Malka and I were separated."

"I think it's nice, Mother, that you had her to talk to," says Olivia.

"Yes, she was the reason I survived. The *real* reason," I say.

"Really?" My daughter is intrigued. So is Dr. Nick, he has been writing on his pad of paper like a madman during the whole session.

"One day Greta left her working spot, she went out into another area. After a while, I started to worry. I couldn't imagine what happened to her, and in a place like Auschwitz, it was easy to think the worst. Eventually, she came back to work. She had the strangest look on her face. 'Where have you been?' I asked her. 'Never mind,' she said. I left it at that. She didn't seem upset or hurt, so I didn't press."

"This kept happening every day. After the first time, I didn't ask her about it. I minded my own business. When she was working next to me she would just chatter like she usually did, so her leaving for an hour or two just became part of the daily routine."

"Well, did you ever find out where she went?" asks Olivia.

"One night, I was eating what the guards called dinner. I usually didn't see Greta other than at morning count and at Kanada, since she stayed in another barrack. I was surprised that she had found me. 'Come with me,' she said, and I followed her to the side of the building. 'I have wonderful news – we're getting out of here!' I couldn't believe what I was hearing. Could this be?" I sip some more tea to cure what's becoming a raspy voice.

"Mother, now is not the time for tea – keep going!"

"Olivia, my throat is dry, for heaven sake!"

"This has to be at her pace, Olivia," says Dr. Nick.

"Sorry. Of course, have some more tea. I feel like I'm finally getting to know my mother, that's all," says Olivia.

"I was so afraid of your reaction. I thought you would disown me," I say.

"Why on earth would I do that? For being a *survivor*?"

"Well, yes," I say. "The guilt and shame I have carried with me for so long, I never thought I would be talking about this with anyone. Now here I am, talking to you, and Dr. Nick, and Malka is here. It's a relief and terrifying at the same time."

"I think that's enough for today," says Dr. Nick. "Nava, you are doing some really good work here. You should be proud of yourself."

36

Nava

I open my eyes to complete darkness. I turn on my side, let my fingers feel their way to the lamp on the nightstand and turn on the light. Malka must have closed my door after I fell asleep. She doesn't know I'm afraid of the dark, so I can't be angry.

As I open my bedroom door I hear the clanking of dishes, the whistle of the teapot and Mozart's *The Magic Flute* playing. I make my way down the staircase and the family is at the table, eating dinner.

"Aunt Nava, sit down," says Lydia. "I have a plate for you, I'll go get it. Roast chicken and all the fixings. You look well-rested, how was your nap?"

"I feel much better, thank you," I say. "What time is it?"

"It's almost eight, Mother," says Olivia.

"Eight – my goodness," I say. "Well, I needed the rest, I guess."

"This is delicious, Lydia," I say. She is a marvelous cook.

"I'm glad you like it." We sat like this for a while, enjoying our food and just being together.

After dinner Malka and I went in the sitting room area of our suite and read by the fireplace. It was a lovely evening.

37

Nava

It is the third day in a row of sessions with Dr. Nick, Malka and Olivia. The sessions are helping, but they are exhausting too. We have all sat down in what has become our usual seating arrangement, and Malka pours tea for everyone.

"I suppose you would like to hear about Greta's plan to leave the camp."

"Of *course* I want to hear about it, Mother," says Olivia. Dr. Nick smiles at me and gets his pen and paper ready.

"All those times Greta left her work area during the day, she was meeting a soldier." I look up at Olivia. "Close your mouth dear, that face is not becoming."

"Sorry, but you said *soldier*, right? An SS soldier?"

"Yes, an SS soldier. I was shocked, I was angry, but I had to put those feelings aside in order to get out of there. As much as you could be a friend in a place like Auschwitz, we were friends. In any friendship there are things about your friend that you don't particularly like. This is the part of her I didn't like. I couldn't comprehend her feeling any type of affection for someone who had a part in the happenings at that camp. I couldn't bring myself to question her, to ask her to justify her feelings and her actions. I had to focus on getting out alive."

"This is unbelievable. Do you think they really cared for each other? Of all places to fall in love, who would have thought."

"There were some inmates that fell in love with each other, but a soldier and an inmate – I couldn't believe it. I don't know if the feelings were real. When I was with them, they seemed like a couple, but like I told you before, my mind was focused on getting out of the camp."

"How did he pull it off?" asks Olivia.

"It was during the day, and Tabbart, that was his name, told us to be silent and let him do the talking. Greta and I sat in the back seat of a Jeep, we drove to the entrance, he showed the guard some paperwork; the soldier looked at us, handed the paperwork back and told him to go ahead."

"Oh, Mother," says Olivia. "I can't believe you were let through. What did the papers say?"

"I don't know what the papers say, but I know that I held my breath from the moment we pulled up to the gate until we passed through it. I was sure my face was turning colors. So relieved, but I could not show any emotion, not yet. Greta trusted Tabbart, but I did not. If I acted happy or like I had victory, he could turn right back around, he could kick me out of the Jeep, he could turn around and shoot me, so I did nothing. Greta and I just stared straight ahead, but we were holding hands, squeezing them tight, sharing a quiet happiness."

"What a story!" Olivia clapped her hands, and threw her head back. "If this is not proof that miracles exist, I don't know what is."

"The whole thing was surreal, one day I am eating cold broth, drinking dirty water, sleeping on bare boards. The next I am in a Jeep on my way to freedom," I say. That memory is clear as day even though I haven't thought about it in many years.

"Why the sad face, Mother? I don't understand."

"People had tried to escape before, several times," I say. "Even with my sense of freedom, I could not help but think of the others. Whenever it was discovered a prisoner had escaped, all the inmates were forced to stand at attention for hours on end, until the prisoner was found. You could not move, you could only look straight ahead."

"How long did everyone stand at attention?" asks Olivia. Dr. Nick is still writing, writing, writing.

"Until the prisoner was found," I say.

"But what if they weren't – oh. That's what you felt guilty about. You knew what the others would go through, right?"

"I remember standing that way, sometimes all day and into

the night. When the prisoner was captured, and they almost always were, they were tortured in front of everyone – unspeakable torture. After that they were hanged, also in front of us. The things I saw, it is too much to think about."

"I'm so sorry, Mother," says Olivia. She pours more tea into my mug and adds the cream and sugar for me.

"Sometimes, if the prisoner was gone a while the guards would get more and more angry. They would start pacing, they would yell at us. Sometimes they would just grab someone at random and start beating. Some were pushed into the open space and shot dead right there. For the first few weeks of freedom, I thought about that a lot. Many days and nights of weeping, knowing I caused people pain and suffering. And Malka, I could picture Malka being beaten, and it broke my heart, that I was the cause of her pain. I wish I had known she had already been transferred to another camp."

"You had to go, Mother. You must realize …"

"Yes, I did. I was eighteen years old. I was free in one sense and trapped by guilt in another sense. I didn't know how to feel about anything, I trusted no one, I was constantly wondering if I would be captured and sent back to the camp. I could see people being tortured in my dreams, so I did not sleep well for years."

"What happened to Greta and Tabbart?" asks Olivia.

"I honestly don't know. I never saw either of them again. We drove for a day and straight through the night. As the sun rose, we went down a long dirt driveway hidden amongst trees. We reached a clearing and I saw a large white farm house with a wrap-around porch. There stood a family, waiting for us. I was introduced to them. Francis and Nina, and their two children, Bert and Helen. Lifelong friends of Tabbart's family. I am not the first Jew they helped. They had heard of the atrocities of the camps and were willing to help when they could. They knew the risks but helped anyway. I stayed with them for almost two years. They were so kind, and I did all I could to earn my keep. I did housework and helped with the children. Even with all of their kindness, I did not trust them completely.

I took everything one day at a time. I would wake up, help prepare breakfast, bathe and clothe the children, do some housework, then it was time for lunch and the afternoon activities, then it was dinner, and reading stories to the children and then bed again. This went on until the end of the war. I was past nineteen when I left that farm. How do you repay a kindness like that? Such special people, so warm and comforting, just what I needed at that time."

"You never saw them again?" asks Olivia.

"No, shortly after I left, I came here to America. I will be grateful for them until my dying day. I am even grateful to Tabbart. He didn't have to take such a risk, but he did, even if it was for Greta's affection, that doesn't matter. The bottom line is, he risked his life for us."

"That's amazing, Mother. I am grateful to him as well."

"I wonder what happened to them, if they went their separate ways, if she used him to get out of the camp or if she really cared for him. Things happened so fast I didn't get a chance to talk to her about it. I guess it doesn't matter. People come in and out of our lives for a reason, good or bad," I say.

"I remember you saying that now and then, and it's so true," says Olivia. "All these years you've kept all that to yourself, that couldn't have been easy. Your strength, it amazes me, but no one needs to be that strong, okay?"

"Again, another great session," says Dr. Nick. "I have a question for both you and Malka. Have you ever thought of going back?"

"To where?" I ask. I look at Malka, and she doesn't seem to understand either.

"To Auschwitz," says Dr. Nick.

38

Malka

"Of course I've thought about it," I say, looking at Nava. "I have been waiting for the right time. I think it's the right time now, to return to the camp. With my sister."

"*What?*" asks Olivia. "Absolutely not!"

"Hold on, Olivia," says Dr. Nick. "Nava, have you ever thought about going back?"

"No," says Nava. "I have spent most of my life trying to erase that time of my life from my mind, and with William I was able to do that. I don't think I could go, Malka. I'm sorry, I can't do it. Maybe Isaac would go with you."

"Think about it, Nava," I say. "Yes, you were able to make a new life for yourself, but since William passed, your memories have returned. You made such leaps at the Museum, don't you think going back would help you?"

"I think it would give her another heart attack," says Olivia, standing. "Maybe she wouldn't survive another one. What you're asking Aunt Malka, is so very selfish. I can't believe you're doing this! Sometimes I wish …."

"What do you wish, Olivia?" asks Dr. Nick.

Olivia sits down and puts her face in her hands. "I don't know what I wish. I just don't know."

"You wish your mother and I hadn't found each other again. You wish I hadn't cluttered up your tidy life, isn't that right?" I ask.

"Don't you put words in my mouth, Aunt Malka." Olivia puts her arm around Nava's shoulders. "Look at her. The mere mention of this trip has drained the color from her face. What are you trying to do, what are you trying to prove here? Please, just go yourself. Go with someone else, anyone else. Please,

don't ask this of her. It's too much, it's just too much, Malka."
Olivia walks towards the door. Her hand on the door knob, she
hangs her head. "I'm sorry, Dr. Nick. I've had enough for
today." And with that, she leaves the room and quietly closes
the door behind her.

"Maybe it would be okay," says Nava, in a whisper.

I look at Dr. Nick. He nods, with a slight grin.

"Sister, do you mean it?" I ask.

"I mean, maybe I'll think about it," says Nava. "Maybe
thinking about it would be okay." She takes a sip of tea. "I think
I have had enough for today as well, if that's all right with you,
Dr. Nick."

"Yes, of course, Nava. We're close to time anyway." He
stands and shakes my hand, and then Nava's. "You are both
doing such great work here, I'm proud of you both."

"Thank you, and you have been a tremendous help," I say.
"We're all very grateful." I show Dr. Nick out after confirming
the next appointment. I close the door and turn around. Olivia
is standing on the staircase, glaring at me.

"What was said after I left the room?" asks Olivia.

"Your mother is going to think about it, Olivia. That's all
that was said."

"She's not actually thinking about going on this trip, is she?"

"Yes, she is," I say, calmly. "And I hope you let her decide
what she wants to do, Olivia. Whatever she decides you should
support her. She needs to come to this decision on her own, all
right?"

"That means you don't influence her either, Malka, okay?"

"Of course not," I say. "We both leave her alone and let her
choose. When she does decide we both accept her answer, no
matter what it is. Deal?"

"Okay, Malka," says Olivia. "It's a deal."

"Great. Let's see if Lydia needs help with dinner."

39

Tim

Hand on the window, she is staring into the clear, sunny sky. "Liv, the plane took off half an hour ago, can we get going?"

She says "Okay," but she doesn't move. She just continues to stare out the window. "I can't believe they actually went. I hope Mother makes it through this trip all right."

"Dr. Krane gave his approval, remember? You were there for the appointment. Dr. Nick is with them if they need him. Try not to worry, Liv." I know I'm wasting my breath.

"Of course I'm going to worry, Tim. Maybe I should have gone too. She wanted me to go, and I had hoped my refusal would change her mind about going. I guess that idea backfired on me."

"They'll be back in a few days, Liv. It's just a few days," I say trying to comfort her. She looks up at me, her eyes heavy with lack of sleep and worry.

"It's what will happen during the next few days I am worried about. Mother is strong in many ways, yet fragile at the same time. I don't know how to explain it."

"I know what you're saying, I do. This is something she felt she had to do, and to be honest I'm quite proud of her."

"When she returns safe and sound I will stop worrying, I promise. I'll be proud, too."

40

Nava

The bus is crowded, people are speaking in soft voices, and I am looking out the window, trying to keep myself calm.

"I think we're here, Nava," says Malka. She takes my hand and gives it a loving squeeze. "We will take it slow, one step at a time, okay honey?"

I smile at my sister. "Okay. One step at a time."

We get off of the bus and I find myself looking only at my sister. I can't seem to look at anything else. Malka is watching me, comforting me with her eyes and her smile and the squeeze of her hands. "Let's go this way," she says. "Just over here, let's walk a little bit."

We begin to walk, following the others. I let myself start to look around, and almost instantly, the weight of the sky, the clouds, the sun – they all become so heavy, like someone has dropped a heavy blanket over all of us.

"There's grass," I say. "And trees. Everything is so colorful."

"Yes, sister," says Malka.

"My memories – all of my memories of this place for all of these years have been in black and white. Now I see color."

"That's good, honey," says Malka. "Let's keep walking."

"Okay, we'll keep walking," I say. Then I see it. I immediately freeze in my spot. It's the main gate. "Arbeit Macht Frei," I whisper.

Malka puts her arm around me and we walk through the main gate. There are trees, tall trees now in color. On the left is the brick administration building, the bricks different shades of reds and browns. I look over to the right, where the orchestra used to play. There is no orchestra there today. No false hope, just a gentle breeze blowing through the tress.

Ahead of us, I see the courtyard in between Block 10 and Block 11, what used to be called "the wall of death." I don't know how many people, naked as the day they were born, stood in front of that wall and were shot dead. I didn't actually see it happen, but all throughout the day people were led in front of that wall and then shot. Standing here, even though there are bundles and bouquets of flowers there in honor of the victims, I can hear those shots so clearly. I close my eyes and shake my head, try to shake the memory out of my mind.

"You okay?" asks Malka.

"I'm okay," I answer. *I'm okay.*

We continue walking a few minutes, in silence. I look around at the people and my heart feels a warmth – they are somber, respectful, and interested. They see what I see now, but they can't see what I saw then. Some of the buildings look the same, but there are also many differences. To our left there are three children playing. They must be four or five years old. I can't help but wonder who would bring children here, to this place, but at the same time I feel a little comfort because I know they will leave this place alive. They are running on the same land millions of people died on, and they don't know it. My emotions are swirling within my mind; I am angry and I am happy that they don't know what I know. They will leave here with happy memories, of playing in the yard. So many children didn't. They didn't leave here at all.

"Look at that," says Malka. Up ahead we see a man kneeling at some kind of monument. He is sobbing, his head in his hands, and he's rocking back and forth. She takes a handkerchief out of her purse and we walk towards him. She puts a hand on his shoulder. When he looks up at her, she offers him the handkerchief. "Thank you, you're very kind," he says.

"Are you all right?" asks Malka.

"No, not really," says the man. He wipes his nose with the handkerchief and then the tears off his cheeks with his sleeve. "Are you two ... survivors?" he asks.

"Yes, we are," says Malka. "We were here a long time ago, when we were teenagers."

The man begins sobbing again. Malka and I look at each other. "I am so sorry," he says. "I am so, so sorry."

"Did you have relatives that were here?" asks Malka. I take a step towards the monument, to read the plaque. I gasp, and look at the man. I realize why he's so upset.

"No," says the man. "Well, yes, I guess I did, but it's not what you think."

"Look at this plaque, Malka," I say. "Read what it says." Malka steps forward and reads the plaque.

"I am so, so sorry," says the man. "A couple months ago I decided to look into my genealogy. I – I am the grandson of this ... this *monster*. He was hung here, after the war, for what he did. I am so ashamed. I'm so *sorry*." He begins to sob louder, and people are starting to walk towards us.

"You are not responsible for what your grandfather did," says Malka. "Dry your eyes and pull yourself together. No one here blames you. Please, tell me your name."

"My name? You want to know my name?" he asks. He looks at me and then back at Malka. He stands up and puts his hands in his pockets, his head hanging in shame.

"Yes, even if you just tell me your first name, God will know who I am praying for," says Malka.

His head lifts, tears streaming down his cheeks. "You're going to pray for me?"

"Yes, of course I am," says Malka.

"Gerard. My name is Gerard." They shake hands.

"It's nice to meet you, Gerard. I will pray for you, pray that you come to terms with who you are related to, and know that he paid for what he did and you don't have to."

"Thank you," says Gerard. He gives Malka a hug. "Thank you for your kindness, and your prayers."

"Of course, Gerard. You keep that handkerchief. I insist," says Malka with a smile.

He turns and gives me a hug as well. "Thank you for your

kindness too."

"You take care," I say to him.

"I'm going to go now. Thanks again," says Gerard, and he walks away.

41

Malka

I am so proud of my sister for coming here. I know it was a hard decision for her to make, and even though she won't tell me, I know she had a hard time convincing Olivia this trip was not only a good idea to come here at all, but also without her. I know I put her in a difficult position, but I wanted to share this with her. It was she and I that were here so many years ago, we need to experience it by ourselves. I don't know how she calmed Olivia down, but she did it, and here we are.

Walking on the camp grounds is incredibly emotional for both of us, maybe even more so for her because she has spent the last fifty years blocking it out and living a completely different life. I have embraced my past and teach others, through the museum, through public speaking and through writing. We are twins, but not identical – we are different on the outside and also the inside.

"Malka, look at this," says Nava. She is ahead of me, by quite a bit. I lagged behind so I could watch her, study her, read her expressions. Her hand is on a glass wall, and behind the glass are thousands of shoes. Shoes and boots of all sizes, styles and colors. Nothing too colorful, mostly black, gray, brown, tan and some white. She is staring at them, as though she is looking for her own perhaps.

Nava has always been a very thoughtful person. She studies, she learns, she makes thoughtful decisions and takes her time doing so. When we were children I found this quality quite annoying, it seemed to take her forever to do anything, but as we grew older, I came to admire this quality. Now I embrace it, sometimes even envy it. Compulsiveness and spontaneity have guided me through much of my life, especially after I met

Joshua, but now the quiet thoughtfulness of my sister is what I want to embrace for myself.

"Malka, look at this," says Nava. Another exhibit, this one contains suitcases and baskets. The suitcases have writing on them, the family name and dates. Again, she is studying them, looking at each one, it seems.

"Malka, are you coming?" she is walking ahead, on to the next exhibit. We see spectacles, clothing, and prosthetic limbs. Each stop she is looking and studying, taking it all in. I wish I could read her mind. She is so brave, my sister. People surround us, stop for a moment look and move on. They look but they don't see. They see a pile of shoes, we see the people wearing them. They see suitcases, we see the people who carried them. They see thousands of spectacles, we see our father put a pair on before he reads us a story. They look, but they don't see.

We come upon a memory wall. There are so many photographs of the victims, wearing their striped uniforms. We look at this wall for a long time as people pass by us, glancing at the photographs. Again, looking but not seeing.

We are outside again, and Nava is walking towards the barbed wire fence. Someone has put a red rose in between the links. Nava walks right up to it and touches the petals. She leans to smell the rose, and then turns to smile at me. "A simple act of kindness in this awful place," she says, and keeps walking.

42

Nava

If someone asked me two years ago if I thought there was a chance I would reunite with my sister and come back to this horrific place, I probably would have looked at them as if they had a dozen heads, all different colors.

It's amazing to me the happenings in my life, especially recently. God answered a thousand prayers when he brought Malka back to me, and I am so grateful. The love I have for my sister knows no boundaries, no one else but her could get me to even consider coming back here, but she did it. She told me to trust her, to let her embrace me in her strength. She has always been stronger than me, physically and emotionally.

As we walk arm in arm, I feel her strength, and I am trying to be strong – for her and for me. We come upon some barracks, and I stop in my tracks. The colors I saw just a moment ago are gone, and I see my mother so clearly, walking around the building up ahead.

"Nava, what is it?" asks Malka. She steps in front of me blocking my view.

"No, Malka, move aside!" She moves a couple steps to the left. "She's *gone*, Malka! I was watching her – why did you *do* that?" I turn away from her, covering my face with my hands. I can't hold them in, they tears escape me.

"Nava, I'm so sorry, who did you see?" she asks, pulling me into her arms.

I pull away and look towards the building. The colors have returned and people are walking about. I am grateful no one seems to have noticed my little outburst. I look at Malka, she looks so worried. "I saw Mother, walking around the building over there. That's the building … the last place I saw her."

"That's the building? Are you sure?" she asks. She takes my hand and we walk towards the building.

"I'm sure, yes. What are you doing, why are we going this way?" I ask.

"Following her steps, sister. Come on," she says.

We walk around the building and there's a small clearing. Before I realize what she's done, it happened so quickly, I realize we are standing in a gas chamber. *Oh, no.* In the center there are some flowers and some small candles lit, making a soft glow. I feel myself starting to tremble. I try to calm myself by focusing on the flame of one of the candles. I take deep steady breaths. There are other people here, and I don't want to make a scene.

Malka lets go of my hand and walks over to one of the walls. It's gray, but there are white streaks all over it. I take a few steps closer. They look like scratch marks made by people trying to escape. I start to tremble again. I close my eyes and I can see myself, standing naked amongst maybe a hundred other naked women. We are scared and screaming when the lights go out for a moment, then come back on. Then, much to everyone's surprise, water comes out – cold water, but water nonetheless. The vision leaves me when I feel a tug on my arm.

"Let's go, Nava," says Malka. "Let's get out of here."

"Yes," I say. "I need to get out of here."

43

Malka

I am woken from a sound sleep by a flight attendant. "Ma'am, please fasten your seat belt, we will be landing shortly."

"Of course," I say. "Thank you." I look at Nava and say, "Thanks for waking me up, I should have said."

"You had a nice rest, sister. I'm glad you were able to get some sleep."

"Did you sleep, Nava?" I ask her.

"Yes, for a little while," she says. "Excited to go home, I guess."

"I'm so glad you went with me, Nava. It really meant the world to me that you came. I'm so proud of you."

"You know I can't say no to you, Malka," she says. We both smile, because we know it's true. "Where is Dr. Nick?"

"Back a few rows," I say. I turn around and see the top of his head. I'm glad he came with us, though we didn't need him too much. He brought his family with him, and they went on a guided tour of the camp. Nava and I wanted to go on our own, and we made the right decision.

"It will be so nice to sleep in my own bed tonight," says Nava. "How long are you going to stay with me in New York?"

"I don't have to rush back to Houston," I say with a smile. "Don't forget we have a Skype date with the family later."

"Looking forward to it," says Nava. "We need to make some plans, maybe see a couple shows? Try a few new restaurants – how does that sound?"

"Sounds like you're happy to be home, sister."

"Very much so. There's no place like home, right?" she asks.

"Click your heels together, we're almost there." I look out

the window and I can see the New York skyline. The city is beautiful at night, everything all lit up, there's nothing like it. I can't help but think of a plaque I saw the other day; it will forever be etched in my mind.

FOR EVER LET THIS PLACE BE
A CRY OF DESPAIR
AND A WARNING TO HUMANITY
WHERE NAZIS MURDERED
ABOUT ONE AND A HALF
MILLION
MEN, WOMEN, AND CHILDREN
MAINLY JEWS
FROM VARIOUS COUNTRIES
OF EUROPE.

AUSCHWITZ – BIRKENAU
1940 - 1945

44

Nava

"Wasn't Olivia supposed to meet us here at the gate?" asks Malka.

"That was the plan, this is so unlike her, to be late for anything," I say. I start to walk around a little bit to see if I can see her anywhere. "So unlike her."

A man in a black suit approaches us, "Excuse me, are you Nava?"

"Yes, I'm Nava, and this is my sister, Malka. Can we help you?"

"Actually, I'm here to help you. I'm here to bring you home," he says smith a smile. "Your daughter sent me."

"Oh, I see. Well, thank you. We still have to get our bags," I say.

"That's fine, I'm here to help with that as well," says the driver.

"Malka, do you think Olivia is all right? I hope nothing has happened. This is so unlike her."

"So you've mentioned," says Malka with a grin. "Maybe something came up with one of the kids, maybe Abbie has a game she forgot about. We'll call her when we get home."

"You don't have your cell phone?" I ask.

Malka shakes her head. "It's back in the suitcase, I didn't think I would need it. It needs to be charged, anyway."

"Okay," I say. "We'll be home soon anyway and we'll get to the bottom of this. I just hope everyone is all right."

"Try not to worry sister," says Malka. "I'm wasting my breath, I know."

SURPRISE!

"Oh, Olivia," I walk into her welcoming embrace. "I

wondered why you weren't at the airport."

"We wanted to welcome you home, Mother, here at the penthouse," says Olivia. Her smile is genuine but tense. "Abbie and I have prepared a welcome home feast, I hope you both are hungry."

"Famished," says Malka. "This was very thoughtful of you all, thank you."

Tim takes the bags and carries them down the hallways towards the bedrooms.

"You'll have to tell us all about the trip, Mother," says Olivia. I know she has been upset with me for going to Auschwitz, she was so against this trip.

"Yes, of course I will," I say. "It's so nice to be home. We have so much to tell all of you."

"You're glad you went then?" asks Olivia.

"I realize now how important it was for me to go," I say. "Malka knew it was what I needed."

"I don't know if you *needed* to go, Mother, but if you are glad you went, then I will try to be glad you went as well."

"I did need to go, Olivia," I say. We sit on the loveseat for a moment. "I needed to go back to see it with older and wiser eyes. Malka calls it closure."

"Malka calls it closure, I call it a risk to your health and well-being," says Olivia. "I suppose Malka and I will never see eye to eye on that."

"Olivia, you were with me when Dr. Krane gave me his consent, remember?"

"Of course I remember." Olivia looks around the room. She looks uneasy, uncomfortable. I wish I could make her understand how important this trip was for me.

"Dr. Nick was with us in case I needed him as well," I say. "Just in case."

"I know all that, Mother. I was worried, that's all. I'm so glad you're home again, safe and sound."

"Of course I am, sweetheart," I say. "Now about that feast you prepared …"

45

Malka

It's been a whirlwind the past few weeks here in New York. Walks in the city, at the park, shopping, Broadway shows, trips to museums and art exhibits. Family dinners and quiet evenings at home with a good book or the newspaper in front of the fireplace. Tonight we return to Broadway to see Phantom of the Opera. Nava can't believe I've never seen it as it's one of her favorites.

"Don't you look pretty, are you ready to go?" asks Nava. "We don't want to be late for our dinner reservation."

"I'm ready, sister. Excited for this evening, to see the show you love so much," I say.

"Oh, I hope you love it, Malka. The music is just – well, you'll see. It's magical."

"Magical? Well, now I really can't wait to see it."

"Come Malka, George has called us a cab."

"I'm coming, I'm coming," I say, grabbing my coat. In the elevator my sister is glowing. I can't stop staring at her, she's radiant.

Walking through the lobby, we are greeted by George. "Your cab is waiting," he says.

"Thank you, George. We're seeing Phantom tonight," says Nava.

"Wonderful! Enjoy your evening you two," he says as he holds the door open for us.

"We will, George, thank you," I say.

Within minutes the cab pulls up to the restaurant, and we are right on time. "Have you been here before, Nava?"

"I haven't. I intentionally picked a new place to try, so we can experience it together," she says with a smile.

"My thoughtful sister," I say. We walk into the restaurant hand in hand, ready for our little adventure.

46

Nava

As I lie in bed looking out the window, I can't help but feel so blessed. The music of *The Phantom of the Opera* is still dancing in my mind. What a treat to see it on Broadway again. Putting on my robe, I start to sway to the music I hear in my mind. I can't stop smiling.

As I cook breakfast, the melody still lingers in my mind and I hum, softly, so I don't wake Malka. Poor thing, she must be exhausted. We have planned more adventures for ourselves, including going back to Broadway to see another one of my favorites, *Les Miserables*. She has decided to stay in New York a couple more weeks, and then I will go with her to Houston for an extended visit there. This is what we've decided to do, as long as we can physically do it.

I glance at the clock, again, and realize it's past the time Malka is usually up and about. Breakfast is ready and waiting for her. I decide to go to her room, hoping to find she is in her bathroom, getting ready for the day.

I open the door and the curtains are closed, the room is still in darkness. I can see she is still sleeping, so I start to leave. I glance back at her once more, and there is something so still about her. So serene and peaceful.

I sit down on the bed, "Malka, time for breakfast, sleepy one." I touch her cheek, and it's cold. I take her hand; it's also cold and it doesn't conform to my own. I gently place my head on her chest to feel her heartbeat. I don't feel anything. "Oh, Malka."

I close my eyes and there we are, running in the field back home, singing and laughing. I trip and we laugh even harder. Malka lies down beside me and we transform the clouds into shapes and share our dreams. We put wildflowers in our hair and run some more, holding hands. We are laughing even more because we're just two silly girls with no worries, only joy.

I open my eyes and reality sets in. I go to the window and open it. "You are free, sister," I whisper. "How I will miss you so."

I return to the bed and sit beside her. I pull the comforter up a little bit, thinking somehow it will make her more comfortable. I put my hand over my heart and think of the irony; my heart attack, the surgery, the long recovery, yet I'm still here. Malka's heart stopped beating, naturally, while she slept. I take some comfort in knowing she didn't suffer. She looks content, as though she is still in the middle of a wonderful dream. I kiss my sister on the forehead and make my way to the living room. I call 911 first, because I need to know for sure my sister has really left me, though the ache in my heart tells me I already know she's gone.

I call Olivia, I need her with me. I am feeling so alone in this big world that truly came alive for me again when my sister came back into my life.

I call Isaac, and tell him how sorry I am, to please tell the rest of the family because I just can't handle more phone calls.

I go back to Malka's room and I kiss her forehead again. "You look so peaceful," I whisper. "Tell William I love him. Tell Mother and Father I will see them again. Tell Isaak ..." I put my face in my hands. "I love you so, my sister. So grateful for the time we had ..." I can't control my tears, and I leave the room.

As I walk down the hallway, there is a knock at the door. "Hello, George. Please come in." Paramedics are behind him and I take them to Malka's room. They confirm what I already know.

"I would like her taken to First Avenue Funeral Services. They handled William and they did a lovely job."

"Yes, ma'am," said a paramedic.

"Mother!" Olivia calls as she enters the penthouse. "Come

here, I am so sorry," she says as she pulls me close to her. She hasn't even taken her coat off yet.

"I called Isaac. I had to tell him his mother is gone," I said as I sit down on the loveseat. I remember the first time Malka was here, she sat beside me on this loveseat, so excited to meet my family. I gave the cushion a pat, and left my hand there, where Malka sat over a year ago.

"Mother, is there anything I can do?" asks Olivia.

"I'm having her brought to First Avenue," I say. "They will do a lovely job, like they did for your father."

"Yes, I'm sure they will. Would you like some tea?"

"No, not right now. Thank you, though." I look up at her, but she is blurry and distorted through my tears. "I'm glad you're here."

The paramedics wheel the gurney down the hall. "We're ready to go, ma'am," says one.

"Yes, thank you," I say, wiping my eyes. "Please be careful with her, she's my sister." I sit back down and hold my face in my hands. "My sister."

"Yes, ma'am. We'll be careful with her. She'll be at First Avenue in a little while."

"Thank you. Thank you very much," I say without looking up.

"You're welcome, ma'am. You take care."

Still not looking up, I nod my head.

"Thank you both," says Olivia. She is sitting close to me with her arm around my back. The door closes, and the paramedics are gone. "I'm going to make some tea."

I can hear Olivia talking on the phone softly in the kitchen. I imagine she has called Tim to let him know what's happened. The house phone starts to ring. Olivia quickly hangs up her cell phone and answers my phone. "Oh, hello, Lydia." I hear her say. "She's here, I'm making her some tea." A pause. "She just left, they're taking her to First Avenue Funeral Services." Another pause. "Well, they handled my father's service and Mother was very pleased with them. It was lovely, they handled everything." This time there was a long pause. "Yes, I understand. Of course, Lydia. We'll see you tomorrow morning. Thank you, see you tomorrow." She gently hangs up the phone and returns to my side.

"Everyone will be here tomorrow."

"All right."

"They have already booked their flight and their hotel rooms. They're all coming."

"All right."

"Mother, they want to bring Malka back to Houston after the funeral, so she can be buried next to Uncle Joshua," says Olivia. "How do you feel about that?"

"Yes, of course. She should be with her husband." I stand up and head down the hallway.

"Where are you going, Mother?" She stands up and begins to follow me.

"I'm going to the kitchen. I'm ready for that tea now."

"Mother, I'll get it for you. Let me get it."

"All right," I say as I sit down at the dining room table. I gently blow into the teacup. The steam twists and turns into the air, my warning not to burn myself. "Perhaps you could put some music on, not too loud."

"Sure, what would you like to hear?"

"Something classical, something to drown out the silence."

There is a knock at the door, and Olivia stands to answer it. "I came as soon as I could," says Tim. "How is she?"

"I'm fine," I say.

"I'm so sorry," he says and gives me an unreturned hug. He exchanges looks with Olivia, I could see it out of the corner of my eye. They are worried; they are concerned. I am numb, empty, and heartbroken. I have no strength to return hugs or even stand up at this moment. My sorrow has weighed me down in this chair, in this room. I keep seeing her on that gurney, in a dark body bag going by me. I wish I had given them a quilt to put over that bag.

"Mother would you like to lie down, or go in the living

room?"

"No."

"Maybe you would be more comfortable in there."

"No."

"Would you like a pastry? You haven't eaten today."

"No."

"Mother, please."

"Please what?" I say and I look up at her.

"Please keep your strength up, please eat, or rest, or do something to take care of yourself."

"I'm fine, Olivia. I want to stay here for now."

"Okay," she says, and I'm happy for the surrender. I have no interest in arguing with my daughter today. "I'll go clean up the kitchen," she says, and Tim follows her out of the room.

I take some more sips of tea and put both hands on the table and stand up.

"Mother?"

"I'm going to lie down, I'm tired."

"Okay, we'll see you in a little while."

I start to pull my drapes shut but stop. Instead, I open them wide and look outside. Down below I see people walking quickly, cars rushing, horns honking. I smile, because I love this city, it has so many memories for me. So much happiness, but I know this is not where I need to be now. I open the window and close my eyes and feel the breeze on my skin.

I climb into bed. I don't think it has ever felt so comfortable. Surrounded by my big fluffy comforter and several pillows, I am face to face with William's picture. "See you soon," I whisper. I pull the picture to my chest and drift into a deep sleep.

CPSIA information can be obtained
at www.ICGtesting.com
Printed in the USA
BVHW03s0437140918
527319BV00005B/76/P